Fragile Embers

STORIES

by Fija Callaghan

This is a work of fiction. Names, characters, businesses, places, events and incidents are either the products of the author's imagination or used in a fictitious manner. Any resemblance to actual persons, living or dead, or actual events is purely coincidental.

Published by Neem Tree Press Limited, 2025
Copyright © Fija Callaghan, 2025

1 3 5 7 9 10 8 6 4 2

Neem Tree Press
An imprint of Unbound
c/o TC Group, 6th Floor King's House, 9–10 Haymarket,
London SW1Y 4BP, UK
www.neemtreepress.com

A catalogue record for this book is available from the British Library

ISBN 978-1-915584-44-1 Paperback
ISBN 978-1-915584-45-8 Ebook

All rights reserved. No part of this publication may be reproduced, distributed, or transmitted in any form or by any means, including photocopying, recording, or other electronic or mechanical methods, without the prior written permission of the publisher, except in the case of brief quotations embodied in critical reviews and certain other non-commercial uses permitted by copyright law. For permission requests, write to the publisher at the address above.

Printed and bound in Great Britain

Frail Little Embers

STORIES

by Fija Callaghan

Neem Tree
Press

Table of Contents

Spinning Sugar	1
Life, Death, and Other Complications	9
To the Waters and the Wild	19
Temperance in a Teapot	27
Dear Audrey	37
Running with Wolves	45
Waking the Witch	59
The Road to Faërie	63
Lost Men	77
An Ephemeral Quality	89
Fox Song	109
Last Wish	119
September Sunsets	123
The Edge of Morning	133
The Selkie and the Swan Maiden	149
After the Fall	153
Apple Seeds	165
The Fleeting Ones	177
Songbird	183
One Hundred Words for Loss	197
The Story Doctor	207
Acknowledgments	225
About the Author	227

Spinning Sugar

The trains that rumbled up to Knaresborough station were rattly, conservatively dressed things, not unlike the people who disembarked there. Nadia watched them from behind the window of her little shop. It was nestled on the open-air platform between the ticket window and a minuscule café that served American-style pancakes.

Most of the people stepping off the train were familiar to her. Many had come in when the shop had first opened, surreptitiously, ashamed of their indulgence, hiding behind words like *the train's running behind is all, won't be a minute…*

It had taken time for the staunch, stalwart Yorkshire people to trust a divorced woman running a business alone, and to trust the silky silver letters spun across a banner the colour of midnight:

La Confiserie des Rêves.

The Candy Shop of Dreams.

Something more appropriate to a city like London, perhaps, than a little train station by the riverside. But the perfume of sticky red fruit and smoky caramel were seductive and, besides, the trains were often late.

Two passengers slipped into the shop. A retired teacher named Charlotte who Nadia knew in passing; she had moved north to be near her daughter, who was studying at a university in Leeds. The other was younger, willowy, unfamiliar, but with something of Charlotte's face around her eyes and nose. A genetic fingerprint that said *you are mine and I am yours*. Nadia fought to steady her breath.

She kept herself unobtrusively occupied as the women perused the displays, which were filled with mostly harmless delights: melon and marigold *pâtes de fruits* to dream of childhood memories; bramble and hawthorn-berry for dreams of lost love. On a delicate glass stand, rose and lemon balm caramels to mend discord as one slept. That had been a difficult recipe to get just right. There were some things even spun sugar couldn't fix.

Charlotte and her daughter leaned over the sparkling array of pâtes de fruits, lined up like jewels in a treasure chest. Pale lemon and elderflower squares through all shades of the rainbow to deep, dark, blackcurrant and clove. Nadia cautioned against eating that one at bedtime.

The younger woman gasped. "These look just marvellous! Do you really make them all yourself?"

Nadia smiled. "I do, yes."

"However did you learn?"

"My grandmother taught me," Nadia said. It had been her father's mother, Mamie Antoinette, who had taught her the art of confectionery. Her mother's mother, Nana Edith, had taught her the other things.

They bought a box of the multicoloured fruit squares to share, and two caramels—maple syrup and tobacco flower, and golden apple kissed with lapsang tea. Later, in the safety of their own beds, in the in-between place just before dreamland, they would remember autumn sunsets and long-forgotten kisses by the bonfire.

"It's very peculiar," Charlotte was saying, as the door drifted shut behind them. "Last month I remember eating one or two of these before bed, and I had the most *extraordinary* dreams."

Nadia broke into the yawn she'd been stifling all day. She couldn't remember the last time she'd properly slept through the night. She shook herself awake and went into the storage room that served as her workshop. A cracked wooden kitchen island housed bowls, jars of light and dark sugars, and the harp cutter that dominated the cramped room. She'd been surprised to learn, years ago, that other confectioners called the stringed slicing apparatus a guitar, in English as well as the French *guitare*. But to Mamie Antoinette it had always been *la harpe*, the harp.

Nadia's husband had never liked the obnoxiously awkward thing taking up space in their kitchen at home. After she had become pregnant she'd used it to slice trays and trays of salmonberry pâtes de fruits with orange blossom and thyme, trying to elicit dreams of the daughter they'd soon be meeting. What would she be like? How would they spend their summers? She didn't tell Julien what she was doing, or how she couldn't understand why she dreamt only of darkness.

She'd heard once that very, very few marriages manage to survive losing a child. By the time Julien left she was already too numb with loss to hear him go. One day there was simply a second hole beside the first, where her daughter and the love of her life should have been.

All she had left were dreams.

From the island she pulled out pots and bowls for the morning's project: pâte de fruit of rosemary and juniper berry. It was the only thing in the shop that brought forth no dreams at all; rather, it welcomed a night filled only with gentle oblivion, sweet shadows that put aside the pain and memories until the light of morning. The recipe had come to her one night as she lay in bed, watching the moon wind its lazy way across the sky.

The ground beneath her feet hummed. The front door rattled as another train pulled up to the platform with a hiss, then stilled under the murmur of voices.

Nadia mixed golden sugar into crushed juniper berries and stirred. The scent tangled itself in her hair. The train had moved on and the station was quiet before she heard new footsteps in the shop.

Sighing, she lifted the bubbling mixture off the heat and stepped out onto the shop floor, pulling the workshop door firmly closed behind her. Slick black loafers clipped against the old floorboards. The shoes met immaculately pressed trousers, then a blazer with broad shoulders that made the compact space look even smaller. He might have been the tallest man Nadia had ever seen. She tried to compare him to Julien in her mind and felt hollow all over again.

"Welcome," she said, brushing her hands on her apron. She had to tilt her head back to look up at him. "Can I be of assistance?"

The man turned, nearly too big for the room, and his shoulder caught the shelf jutting from the wall. The stand with the rose and lemon balm caramels shuddered, then leapt. Glass exploded on the wooden floor.

"Oh gosh, I'm terribly sorry." The man knelt down and hit his head on the shelf. He muttered something slightly more colourful than *gosh* and put his hand to his head. "Sorry. Really."

Nadia bit back a smile. Julien had sworn like a sailor. "Don't worry. I'll fetch the dustpan." She manoeuvred against the large man, rustling his blazer, and retrieved the small brush from behind the counter. The caramels had been on their way out, anyhow. She'd tried one earlier that day to see if it was getting too dry.

"So, what can I help you with?" she asked, as she swept up the glass shards and the caramels. Even in their wrappers, the ethereal scent of lemon balm and rose reached for her, caressed her, whispered stories of forgiveness and peace and mornings full of promise. She brushed it impatiently away.

"I was looking for something to bring my daughter." The man looked around at the glittering confections. "She's been having bad dreams."

Nadia looked up, startled. "Oh?"

"Yeah. I thought a nice surprise would help her rest a little easier. You must know what children are like."

She bit her lip. Not trusting herself to speak, she just shook her head.

She put the dustpan and brush away and wandered over to the pâtes de fruits. A few of the last batch of juniper berry were left. Certainly they would help still the nightmares. Or perhaps loganberry and sea salt, for dreams of languid summer days by the sea.

"How old is your daughter?" she heard herself asking. Hers and Julien's would have been three now. Three last month.

"She's three," the man replied. Nadia glanced over sharply. "And you?" he asked, "have you any children of your own?"

She hesitated, her fingers on the worn wood countertop. It wasn't the first time someone had asked her that. *Consider yourself lucky*, a local woman had said, grinning at the gangly preteen she dragged along behind her. They both knew she didn't mean it.

"Almost."

When she'd felt the sharp snap in her stomach and the wet between her legs, she thought she was going into labour. She looked around for Julien. Then she saw the blood.

"I see," the man said. And he did, somehow. He saw everything. "What was her name?"

It didn't occur to Nadia to wonder how he knew it was a her. It seemed as natural as her own understanding that it was a daughter that grew inside her.

"Anne," she said. After Julien's grandmother. Nadia liked it because it sounded like her own grandmother too, Antoinette. "She nearly made it. It was almost time, but she…*I*…wasn't strong enough."

The man stepped towards her. He smelled of Julien's aftershave, and roses. Roses and lemon balm. The tears in her eyes made the sharp lights blur.

"Strength has nothing to do with it. It wasn't her time yet. She knew it and just didn't know how to tell you."

"But I miss her," Nadia whispered. Everything she could have been. Their family. The life they would never have. She wrapped her arms around herself and was surprised to see that her fingers were bloody. She looked at them curiously. They smelled like strawberries. Strawberry was Julien's favourite.

"Of course you do. She misses you too. And you'll see her again one day, after you've lived a long, full life. But you've got to live it first. You need to collect all the stories you're going to tell her."

She squeezed her eyes closed, willing herself to stay standing. Tears escaped and rolled down her face. One sank into her lips. It tasted of sugar-water.

Nadia opened her eyes. The man wasn't as tall as she'd thought, or maybe it was the shop that wasn't so small. The corridor stretched out past the train tracks, over the river, out beyond the confines of North Yorkshire and towards Mamie Antoinette's garden in Fontenay-aux-Roses. The *confiserie* was the entire world.

The man brushed a tendril of hair out of her eyes, just as Julien had done so, so many times. Her heart broke all over again.

"It's okay, Nadia," Julien said. "It's okay to start living."

He might have said something else. She wasn't sure. Whatever it was became lost in the rumble of the next train.

The light hurt her eyes. She had fallen asleep awkwardly at her work table, sitting on something that might have generously been called a bar stool or, less generously, a small coat rack. Something crinkled in her hand. It was an empty sweet wrapper, still smelling of lemon balm and rose.

She came out to the front of the tiny shop, staggering on legs that hadn't quite woken up all the way. The glass stand piled with caramels still stood on the shelf, glittering invitingly. She decided she'd give the caramels a few more days.

Nadia went to the front door and looked out. The air was cool and fresh. A train idled on the platform and commuters passed in and out. Some of them waved to her.

Once the train pulled away, Nadia retrieved her keys and locked up the shop. Just beyond the hill the River Nidd sparkled. It was a lovely day for a walk.

Life, Death, and Other Complications

Whitman's twenty-four-hour bookshop was tucked into a narrow brick alley just off West Collins. It had a kettle, a coffee machine, and extra blankets, and nobody was ever turned away.

Tom O'Connell had started coming to Mr Whitman's bookshop when he'd arrived in America and found it wasn't quite the gold-paved land of opportunity he'd been led to believe. When Mr Whitman passed away at the turn of the millennium, Tom took over running the place. He managed sales during the day and kept the shop open as a lending library while he slept in the little attic room at night. Mr Whitman still checked in from time to time, mostly just after twilight and near the old high cross-quarter days. Sometimes he made coffee. It was scorched and noxious, like all dead food, and Tom had to throw it out and make a fresh one when Mr Whitman wasn't looking.

He didn't mind the old man, though. He knew how hard it could be, sometimes, to let go.

Tom was checking his email when the snow started. Mr Whitman didn't like computers and kicked up a terrible fuss when Tom first tried to get one for the office. Then Tom told him he was behaving like a poltergeist, and Mr Whitman didn't speak to him for a week. A few days later he found a flyer on the desk advertising reduced prices on monthly broadband.

He scrolled through a message requesting space rental for a poetry slam, a promotional email advertising website maintenance (he didn't have a website), and a CV from someone looking for a job. He went to grimly delete it—there was never any money in bookshops, especially ones that stayed open all night—then stopped as he saw the name: Mairead Ryan. Not one he had ever come across in America, though it wasn't uncommon back home. The message had been sent several days ago. He closed the screen instead.

"Might not be such a bad idea, taking on some help." The voice came from somewhere in the stacks.

Tom sighed. "There isn't any money. Some of us still need it to eat and pay our rent, you know."

Mr Whitman let the subject drop. Tom did a round through the bookshop—larger than it looked, with three cramped floors and a sign that said, "Warning: floorboards unstable" on the top one. The winter's chill had brought in a handful of people looking to escape the cold. They nestled into corners behind well-worn books, shoulders hunched as they tried to make themselves smaller. These were people used to being thrown out of every corner of the world they tried to occupy simply for existing. Some were familiar faces, like Maggie, who couldn't keep up her mortgage payments after her husband of twelve years left her for another woman; or Jamie, who had been just on the brink of finishing his screenplay for the last three years. Some faces were new, grateful for a little peace and warmth before disappearing back into the tapestry of the world.

When Mr Whitman had been alive and Tom had been his assistant, part of his job had been to go around and offer people coffee or tea. He remembered the way their shoulders would tense as though bracing for a reprimand or worse, how they'd start throwing things into bags in a long-honed practice of needing to leave quickly. Then the gratitude in their eyes once they realised they weren't unwelcome, that someone was showing them kindness, was so raw and naked that it made him turn away. He thought about the lattes he'd devoured through uni without even tasting them and felt sick.

The next winter, Mr Whitman had a stroke at the bottom of the stairs. Tom never left.

"I'm just putting the kettle on," Tom announced loudly. "Would anyone like a cup of tea?" He'd learned that people were less hesitant if he was already making something for himself.

A few of the readers nodded shyly, and he went back downstairs to the little kitchenette.

"That was kind of you," a voice behind him said. It wasn't Mr Whitman's voice. Tom turned around.

An auburn-haired woman in a smart black dress and coat smiled and glanced up the stairs. Voices carried easily through the old wood. She obviously wasn't sleeping hard; maybe an artist or a writer, the kind that stayed up scribbling into sketchpads and notebooks long after the cafés were closed. Snowflakes dusted her shoulders.

"It's nothing." Tom found himself unexpectedly shy. "Do you want something? A tea or a coffee? I think there might be some hot chocolate mix around. It's not very good, though."

"Well maybe a tea then, if you're already making it."

He finally registered her accent. "You're Irish?" he said in surprise. His own had softened over the years. Since arriving in the States, he'd never gone back.

"I am, yeah. Just moved here. Can I give you a hand with the tea?"

Mr Whitman was hovering. Tom could almost see him, just beyond the edges of his vision.

"She's quite pretty, isn't she?" Mr Whitman said.

"Oh, be quiet," said Tom, and then nearly bit off his own tongue.

The woman flushed. "Sorry. Never mind."

"No, I wasn't talking to you. I mean, I was talking to myself." He waved a hand towards his head, as though to indicate the offending party. "Yeah, no, it's just boiling water at the minute. Just waiting for the light to go off." He pointed at the blue indicator light.

"She's Irish, you dumb brick, she knows how a kettle works."

Tom turned his back to Mr Whitman, approximately.

"What kind of tea do you take?" he asked. "We've black and peppermint. And there's milk." He shuffled around the kitchenette, pulling out teabags and paper cups.

"Black tea with milk would be lovely. I'm Mairead, by the way."

"Oh, *you're* Mairead?" he said. Her smile broadened.

"Yes, I sent you a CV last week. That's actually why I'm here. I'm out looking for a job."

"Not for the finest bottom-shelf cuppa in town, then?" he teased. His own familiarity caught him off guard.

"Well, I've only just arrived. I'm discovering all of the city's finest for the first time."

Somewhere in the shop, Mr Whitman was humming. It sounded suspiciously like Frank Sinatra.

"How long have you been over for?" he asked.

"Just three weeks. How about yourself?"

"Eight years. Going on eight years." He tore open the tea envelopes. One tore right through the teabag, so he had to toss it out and get another one.

"It's gone well for you, then? I mean, if you've stayed that long."

He wasn't sure how to answer that. "It was…it wasn't quite what I thought it would be. I guess nothing ever is, though. What about you, how are you finding it so far?"

She hesitated and wrapped her jacket tighter around herself. "I didn't know it would be so cold."

He smiled wryly. "You get used to that."

"And people are a bit…sometimes they're kind of…mean."

"Yeah, you get used to that too."

She laughed. "I was surprised when I heard your accent. It's nice to hear something from home." She flushed. The snowflakes had melted and now her hair was dotted with tiny drops of water.

He wasn't sure when Ireland had stopped feeling like home to him. It had happened so gradually that he hadn't even noticed. But then, this city didn't feel like home either, with its frigid winters and its cranky commuters who drove on the wrong side of the road. Maybe the bookshop was the closest thing to a home he had. The cramped attic bedroom upstairs. This little kitchenette. The thought made him feel hollow.

"So, what is it you're here looking for?" he asked. "The great American dream?"

"What makes you think I'm looking for something?"

"Everybody who comes here is looking for something."

"I don't know. I've always wanted to work in a library. I got a master's in library sciences, but there weren't any jobs back home, and I'd heard all these things about people who went to America…" Mairead looked at her feet. "I guess I thought there would be a place for me."

Tom sighed. He'd arrived with a master's degree in computer science, at the dusk of the '90s when they were still met with a mix of suspicion and intrigue. Running from a broken relationship and a suffocating Catholic family, he'd thought the entire world would be at his feet. Then he'd watched his expensive degree and his ideals get sloughed away down the great American drain.

"You're quite brave," Tom said.

"Well, so were you."

He shrugged. "I was. A long time ago."

The kettle clicked off. He poured water into the paper cups. Steam rose into the air.

"What's that smell?" Mairead asked suddenly.

Tom sniffed the air and groaned. While he'd been distracted, Mr Whitman had helpfully made some coffee. He took the lid off the pot and a cloud of thick, sludgy despair floated up. He replaced the lid with a thwack.

"I must have left it for too long. Here, maybe you could bring these to the people upstairs." He handed her the tea. "I'll start a new one."

She took the hot cups and, balancing them precariously, headed up the stairwell. Tom set about scrubbing out the coffee pot.

"Oh drat, did it burn?" Mr Whitman's voice came from right beside his ear.

Tom wanted to smack him. "It's alright, it's easy to do." He poured the coffee down the drain and held his breath, but a few of the fumes made their way in. They whispered to him of lost dreams, of missed opportunities, of festering regrets. He shook them off and ran fresh water from the tap on high.

"Seems like a nice girl, that Mairead. Funny name though."

Tom sighed. "Yeah, a nice girl."

"She's from Wexford too, you know, just like you."

"How the hell could you know that? When we first met you thought I was English."

"I looked in her purse."

Tom closed his eyes and counted to ten. "You can't just go looking in women's handbags."

"Oh hush, I wasn't doing any harm. She's twenty-eight and her middle name's 'Brighid'. With a D at the end."

"Just…" Tom gritted his teeth as he scrubbed the coffee pot clean. "Leave it. And stop looking in people's handbags."

"And I'm the stubborn one, am I? You have a real chance delivered right to your doorstep and you won't even look up from the damn coffee." The faucet sputtered and spat out rusty water, making Tom jump.

"She's here for a job, you nit, not a…complication."

"Moving to the States was a 'complication'. Every goddamn day is a 'complication'. *That's what it is to be alive.*"

"And what could you possibly know about it?" Tom snapped. "You haven't been alive for years." His voice was getting louder. He hoped Mairead couldn't hear him.

Mr Whitman said nothing. Tom wondered if he had stormed off to whatever ether he occupied.

He turned the faucet off.

"We're both dead, son," said Mr Whitman's voice quietly. "We're both haunting this place. I'm just more honest about it."

Tom suddenly felt very tired. "What does that mean?"

"Look at me," Mr Whitman said. "I lived my whole life here. I never married. I never did anything worthwhile. I couldn't see what a gift life was until it was taken away from me."

"That's not true. You gave people hope. You created a safe place. You saved people."

"I gave people a place where they could save themselves. Fine. That's not the point. I held on so tight that I didn't know how to live, and then when I died I was still holding on so tight I couldn't even do that properly. I don't want that for you."

"But you're still here because you want to be," Tom said impatiently.

There was silence.

"Aren't you?"

Mr Whitman said nothing.

Tom stared down at the coffee pot in his hands. The glass was worn ragged from all the times he'd used scouring pads to get out Mr Whitman's decrepit coffee. All those years he'd assumed that Mr Whitman didn't trust him to take care of things on his own, that he was checking up on him to make sure he didn't screw up or run the bookshop into the ground. He'd never thought about what Mr Whitman wanted. He'd never even asked.

"I'm sorry. I didn't know."

"It doesn't matter." Mr Whitman's voice was thick and watery. "What matters is that you still have a shot at a real life. Maybe it'll be with Mairead Brighid up there, or maybe it'll be with someone else, but if you don't start living soon, you never will. Don't make the same mistake I did."

Tom flicked on the coffee maker and poured fresh ground coffee into the top. His hands felt like lead. Mairead had been gone a long time. Maybe she'd heard him talking to himself and left.

He went up and found her chatting easily to the group of people upstairs. Maggie and Jamie were smiling, looking lighter and more at home than he'd ever seen them. Mairead stood when she saw him and joined him in the hall. The cheerful murmur of chatter mingled with the dusty smell of old books.

"I don't have any jobs to offer," Tom said. "And with your qualifications, you could do a lot better than this. But I could put the word out to some of the bigger bookshops and see if they need any help over the holidays. It would be a start, anyway." He stuffed his hands in his pockets, feeling useless.

"That'd be grand, thank you." Her smile lit up the narrow hall.

Tom looked down at his shoes. They were falling apart. "And if you're ever stuck, or you just need something to come home to, you know, you can always come here. It's not luxury or anything, but it's a safe place." He met her eyes. "You're not on your own."

"Thank you." This time it came out as a whisper. Her smile played cautiously around her lips. "That's really good to know." She held his gaze a moment longer, then looked away and put down the paper cup. "And for the tea."

She gave him a little wave as she pulled open the shop door and disappeared into the deepening twilight.

Tom stood in the doorway a minute longer and watched the falling snow. From somewhere far away, like a breath on the wind, he could hear Mr Whitman humming.

To the Waters and the Wild

The baby had been left at the very edge of the tide, wrapped in a blanket of sealskin, moored on shells and stones as the waves pulled away. This must have been when I'd first become aware that my mother was not the same woman who gave birth to me—though I never knew that Other Mother, not her face nor even her name—because my first thought was that they'd brought me to the shore in trade. That they would take my new baby sister and I would be the one left behind.

They didn't, though. My mother bundled up my sister in her sealskin, and placed her free hand in mine, and took us both home.

I remember little after that, except that we moved far, far inland where the sea could not reach us. It would be many years before I saw it again.

My mother locked the sealskin blanket away in an oakwood trunk.

They called her Aoife, "radiance", in spite of her dark eyes and dark hair. Later I would come to understand that my mother could not bear children of her own, but somehow she ended up with two—one born of the wind and waves, and one born of her husband's touch on another woman's skin. I have pictured it often, my father coming home with a swaddled child still streaked in his dead mistress's birthing blood. *I couldn't just leave him*, he might have said. And my mother: *I'll put the kettle on*.

I don't know if it really happened like that. But I do know that many men would have walked away and left their bastard son to die in the Other Mother's arms. My existence is its own tiny miracle.

When we moved inland, Aoife went to the girls' school and I to the boys' nearby. I tell myself that's why I didn't see how bad things got for her though, looking back, I should have. Aoife was an easy target for the malice of young girls. She learned to speak late, and when she did, spoke seldom; and despite the cotton gloves our mother bought for her, it wasn't long before others saw the thin, iridescent webbing that stretched between each slender finger. The nuns once tried to cut it out, but Aoife screamed and bled so profusely that they left it alone. She told our mother her hand was bandaged because she'd caught it in the woodstove. It was only later, when the house was dark and quiet, that she told me the truth. Some of it, at any rate.

But what could I have done? I was only a child.

We love to say that, don't we? *I was only a child*, as if children don't see and hear more clearly than we do, as if they can't slip through cracks adults have long since outgrown. Perhaps I could have done more. Instead, I pulled away, preoccupied with my own day-to-day battles and discoveries. First: lizards in the rivers, pebbles shot through with veins of quartz, new hiding places in the treetops with the other boys. Later: cigarettes and clumsy kisses with a schoolmate's sister, reusing the treetop hideaways for other things. Clumsy kisses with the schoolmate. Learning to never be the smallest or weakest person in the room.

I was sixteen and Aoife twelve when our father was struck by a passing lorry. I walked to Aoife's school as I did each day, where we would wait for our mother or father to come in the motor car and take us home. We waited. No one came.

They took his body away before either of us had a chance to see it. Our mother pulled us both into a tight embrace and wouldn't let go, even when we began to struggle against her. A brief moment of panic, then slender Aoife was able to slip out, and there was suddenly room to breathe, and I slipped out too. My mother's nails scraped my skin as I escaped.

The following summer, several lads were invited to spend a week at a mate's family's cottage by the sea, which would be empty and unobserved. I didn't ask; I simply told Mother and Aoife I was going. I turned away from my sister's pleading eyes.

Now they are developing medicines for people like my mother—people whose sickness is not in the body, but in the mind. But in those days there was still so much we did not understand.

I walked the shoreline and tasted the sea salt of my childhood, those four fragile years before we stumbled on baby Aoife in her sealskin, before my mother began running, running, always running from something for which she had no name. Perhaps she knew what it takes so many of us a lifetime to learn: to love and be loved is to have something to lose. She had finally found the family she'd always wanted, which meant from that day forward she was fighting to outrun the moment she would lose it all.

Perhaps. Or perhaps she simply knew enough old stories to recognise Aoife for what she was. There is no love strong enough to chain the sea.

A fire burned, and meat was smoked and stolen liquor passed between friends as we played at being men. None of us liked each other very much, but we clung together because it made the world seem a little less frightening than if we were alone. I can admit that now. Back then, I'm sure I'd have sworn to lay down my life for them. The smoke seared my eyes and made me cough.

And I thought, guiltily, of Aoife, her pleading stare, my mother's protective arm pulling her close. That's when I stood, leaving the gathering behind and letting the night swallow the edges between my body and the world. And somewhere around the time the shouts and laughter were buried by the waves, I saw a boy. He was sitting cross-legged, using a stick to draw pictures in the sand.

He looked up at my approach, and our eyes met.

I am hesitant, here, to place too much trust in memory. I'm never sure how much was waking and how much was dreaming, or how much I added later to impose clarity and order on shadow. I recall words, but not who spoke them. I recall cold hands on hot skin. I recall taking one of those hands in mine and seeing the thin, iridescent webbing between each finger, and realising suddenly that Aoife never should have been taken from this place. We were selfish.

I watched through slitted eyelids as he stood and wrapped himself in a slick grey coat. Then the sea took him. In that moment I finally understood.

A seal crested the waves, then slipped away into darkness.

When I arrived home, Aoife had dark blue marks on her upper arm and a corner of the kitchen had caught fire. I pulled her into my arms, something I had done perhaps twice across thirteen years. She held me too.

"I forgive you," she whispered.

My mother did not forgive so easily. She took to her bed and muttered that my father had left her, that I had left her, but Aoife never would. Aoife would never leave her. She said it again and again until I felt sick.

The next day, when Mother and Aoife went to the marketplace, I attacked the oakwood trunk with kitchen knives. The key, I suspected, had disappeared long ago; but the trunk was old, and the mechanism unsophisticated, and before long I had pulled the lock apart. I hid the sealskin blanket beneath my bed until morning.

Did I know, then, what the price would be? Some part of me must have understood that, in the end, only one of us could be free.

We both woke with the first grey glimmers of dawn. I handed Aoife a bag with her sealskin, bread and fresh water, and money for the train. There were too many things to say, apologies and promises jostling for space in a moment that grew smaller and smaller with every breath.

I'm sorry I wasn't a better brother, I might have said.

I'm sorry I didn't understand sooner.

I'm sorry I didn't protect you.

And Aoife: *I forgive you*.

She was gone by the time the first rays of sunlight crested the horizon.

The doctor has been once today already, but he's come again to tell me I should prepare to say goodbye. A symphony of illnesses plays inside my mother's lungs. I'm not sure how to feel about it. I do love her, this broken woman who took in her husband's son so many years ago. Something like love, anyway.

She turns in her bed and reaches for my hand. I uncross my legs, old and stiff, and let her find it. Hers feels like scorched newsprint.

"You'll never leave me, will you darling?" she says. I can't tell if she's awake. It may not even be me she's talking to.

"Never," I assure her, and run my thumb over hers. "I will never leave you." I will say it again and again until the end. And then, at last, it will be my turn to give myself to the sea.

Temperance in a Teapot

An old superstition said that if two people poured from the same teapot, they were bound to have an argument before the day was through.

That was never the case with Rhyms teapots, which had been made for generations by the Rhyms family in their home on the River Breer. Everyone knew that a teapot with the Rhyms stamp on it—a classic gift for weddings, christenings, and new business ventures—always kept tea at the perfect temperature, and always ensured that lingering quarrels seemed smaller and sillier than they had before. After all, there was nothing more comforting than a shared pot of tea.

It was Nora Rhyms who first thought of opening a tea room adjacent to the pottery workshop. That way, people who couldn't afford a Rhyms teapot of their own could at least share the experience with a loved one for an afternoon. A tiny retail section housed the coveted teapots and their own line of house-branded loose-leaf tea. Nora had a good head for business, and what could have disappeared into the collective archive of Irish countryside novelties became a beloved twenty-first century institution.

And while Nora handled the accounts and the maintenance and social media marketing and ordering pastries from the next town over and training a local girl to serve at lunchtimes, Nora's husband Frédéric learned how to make teapots.

Frédéric had been raised by two *pâtissiers* and, he explained, working with *pâte sucré* was not all that different from working with clay. Nora loved watching him in the workshop beside her father, coaxing the wet clay around the wheel and smoothing it into shape with his strong, warm hands. Now that Nora's brother Niall had gone off to New Zealand, her father was grateful for the help. Frédéric was the first non-Rhyms man to work with Breer river clay in more than seventy years.

Nora was tidying the café just after teatime, and she had the idea of putting a window into the wall between the tea room and the workshop so that people could watch the teapots being made. Tourists loved that sort of thing. So she went across to the workshop to ask Frédéric and her father what they thought of the idea, and was shocked to find them in the midst of a heated argument.

Nobody in the Rhyms family ever had arguments.

They broke off when they saw her. Her father nodded to Nora and brushed past her, muttering, "Bloody Frenchmen" under his breath.

Nora turned to Frédéric, but he simply shrugged and dried his hands on a mottled, clay-stained tea towel.

Later, as they lay in bed watching the moonlight filter through the window, Nora asked him what they'd been fighting about.

"Your father is…how do you say…an old lion. He likes his ways."

"Oh?" Nora didn't think her father was like that. "How so?"

He turned to her, silhouetted against the moon. "I said to him we should make also the teacups and the…*sous-tasse?*"

"Saucers."

"Yes, the saucers as well. The teapots are beautiful, but they are only one product for an entire *enterprise*. But he said no."

"We used to make them," Nora said. "I mean, not us. My grandfather and his parents did. I see them sometimes on eBay."

"Why did they stop?"

Nora turned to lie on her back. "I think because there's only so much clay along the river. Once we use it up, we can't make any more."

"So they bring clay from another river. There are many in France. It is simple." He said this as though it solved everything.

Finally Nora understood what the argument had really been about. "There aren't many like this one," she said quietly. Rhyms teapots were special because they came from the Breer. Nowhere else.

Frédéric was unconvinced. "The *terroir* is important, yes, but so is the business. If my parents cannot buy chocolate from Madagascar because of the rains, maybe they need to order from Venezuela, or Côte d'Ivoire."

Nora sighed. She knew Frédéric was only trying to help, but he wasn't a Rhyms. He couldn't understand.

The next day Nora was running the tea room on her own, since her serving girl was away visiting family in the west, and her hands were being uncharacteristically clumsy. Before three o'clock she'd already broken two teacups—not the precious teapots, thanks be, but an annoyance all the same. Earlier, a man had proposed to his girlfriend over tea. Though Nora couldn't exactly ban them outright, proposals in the tea room made her uneasy; it felt too much like coercion. No one ever said no over a Rhyms teapot.

She had said no to Frédéric the first time he asked her, after her summer abroad drinking in light and life on the coast of France, because it was too fast, too surreal, and surely he wouldn't leave sunny Montpellier behind for a windswept, ramshackle pottery shed. But then, after a long winter of old-fashioned handwritten letters, he'd come to visit her and her family that past spring. The second time he asked her she said yes.

Now Nora cleared crockery from empty tables as two lingering women, perhaps a mother and a daughter, whispered fervently across their teapot. Nora was used to gossiping ladies, to unexpected camaraderie loosening secrets long buried—usually with a smile and a guilty, wistful sigh. But something didn't look quite right about this. The younger woman was flushed with anger or embarrassment, and the elder spoke in a low, heated voice.

Had Nora been any other woman, from any other family, she might have said the women were having an argument. But that was ridiculous. A Rhyms teapot (a classic gift for weddings, christenings, and new business ventures) brought only harmony. Only tranquillity and love.

The younger woman pushed back her chair with a determined scrape, swung her handbag over her shoulder, and left the tea room. Nora gawped.

She hurried over, dishcloth in hand.

"How did you find everything? The tea quite alright?" She smiled in the carefree way one only did in service, hiding her churning insides.

The woman heaved a big sigh. "Oh yes, lovely, thank you. Just silly stuff." Her smile mirrored Nora's own, bright and insubstantial as a flash of sunlight on the Breer. "You have children yourself?"

"I've my husband," Nora said. "I couldn't handle any more childminding than that." She didn't mind Frédéric really, but it was the sort of joke women enjoyed sharing together.

The woman rewarded her by dropping some of the tension from her shoulders. She smiled a bit more warmly and handed Nora a twenty-euro note. "Well, best to you."

As soon as she was gone, Nora eyed the teapot suspiciously. The only explanation was that they hadn't poured any tea. They'd ordered it, and then they'd got into a tizzy before they'd got round to drinking it.

She lifted the lid and peered inside. The pot was two-thirds empty.

After she finished clearing the last tables and cashing up the register, Nora met Frédéric at the pottery so they could walk home together. The two of them had moved into Niall's cottage after he'd left, since it was bigger than the studio flat Nora'd lived in before, and that way they could keep it from falling to ruin before Niall came back from New Zealand. She and Frédéric walked along the dusty road in the late-afternoon sun, Frédéric shuffling so he wouldn't outpace her with his long, loping strides.

She debated telling him about the argument in the tea room, but she wasn't sure he would really grasp why it was worrisome. *Always children and parents argue*, she imagined him saying. *C'est normal.*

Her father would understand immediately, but just as quickly he'd leap to blame Frédéric. Worse, Nora wasn't sure he'd be wrong.

The terroir is important, yes, but so is the business. And so were the hands that shaped the clay, the generations of feet that splashed through Breer river water, the memories Nora held close of her and Niall watching herons stretch their pewter wings. Terroir was so much more than choosing the right soil with the right minerals. Terroir was in their blood.

"I was thinking," Frédéric broke into her thoughts, "many pâtisseries in France now sell teas and coffees and gift things. Perhaps we could send some teapots to my parents, and also some of the teas and they could sell them there. And then maybe we could grow the Rhyms brand to be famous in other countries, too."

Nora hesitated. "I don't know if people in France…I mean, we would have to explain what's special about them and why they're so expensive. They're not something you just buy off the shelf."

Frédéric waved her cares away. "The wealthy who come there from Paris, for them the price is not important. For the prestige, they will pay."

And there wasn't enough clay, Nora wanted to add, to be famous in other countries. But they'd had that conversation once already.

"I'll talk to my father," she said instead.

─✦─

Since they closed the tearoom on Mondays, and Frédéric was finishing firing that weekend's production, Nora left their house and went for a walk. Her feet took her past the familiar little village and to the rugged edge of the River Breer.

Her earliest childhood memories were of scraping mounds of clay from the riverbed with her bare hands, kneading them and filtering them through layers of cheesecloth until smooth. Her father had asked Niall to show her how to do it and Niall, only three years older, had leapt at the chance to prove his superiority. Yet he was always patient with her and together they would lug the buckets home for their father to spin into shape. But now the tea room kept Nora so busy that she hadn't come to the river in months. Not since before Frédéric became a part of their family.

There was a saying she'd heard once, in school: you never step in the same river twice. While she could appreciate the sentiment, in practice she thought it was nonsense. The Breer burbled along gently, the same as it had when she was a little girl. Even as the towns around it changed, as the cottages fell to the axe of new apartment complexes and dirt roads collapsed beneath slick new paving, the river remained unchanged.

Nora knelt at the water's edge and reached through the ripples to the cool soil underneath. She pressed the silt and sand between the pads of her fingers.

She had thought, when Frédéric left Montpellier, that he would come to be happy here. But she could feel his restlessness, his need to make himself more useful, more seen, to fill a space that was both too big for him and too small.

She let the soil fall back into the water and stood up. The river continued to flow, unbroken.

～⚜～

"My parents are asking when we are going to come to Montpellier," Frédéric said, "to visit."

Nora had met Frédéric's parents on exactly two occasions: after she'd accepted his proposal, and then again on their wedding day. Of the two of them, his mother spoke the better English—because, she told Nora confidentially, of *les soap opéras*—and his father spoke little, but always with a warm smile.

Nora glanced up from the stovetop, where she was cooking their dinner. "I'd be delighted," she said carefully, "but I don't know when we'd be able to. I can't close the tea room, and my father needs me here." She didn't realise until after the words left her mouth that she'd said "me", not "us".

She glanced at Frédéric and saw that he'd noticed too.

He came and joined her at the stove. "Well, perhaps I could go, only for two or three days. Maybe show them your teapots also."

"You could take one as a gift," Nora said. "One you made with your own hands. They'd love it, I'm sure." But an uneasy feeling settled in her stomach.

"Yes, *peut-être*," he said softly, and Nora glanced at him. He looked as though his thoughts had turned somewhere else. She was struck by the gentle curl of his hair around his ear, the sharp line of his jaw softened by day-old stubble, this strange and beautiful love that had blown so suddenly into her life.

The uneasiness in her stomach sharpened, and she recognised it for what it was: a deep, visceral knowledge that if he left the village without her, he would not come back.

***

Frédéric would take the train and then the ferry to France, guarding the precious teapot close at hand. Nora walked him to the station, tucking her hand in his. His fingers were softer than they'd been when they had first met, worn smooth by clay. As they arrived, he turned to face her.

Nora ran her thumb over his. "*Bon voyage*," she said weakly.

"*Bon courage*," he returned. "Are you certain you will not join me?"

She hesitated. She remembered his letters, always smelling faintly of coffee. His strong hands, shaping teapots on the wheel beside her father. How the first time she lay beside him and noticed dried clay under his fingernails, it felt like coming home. The first non-Rhyms man to work with Breer river clay in more than seventy years. Did he know, Nora wondered, what he was truly asking? Or would he only see it once he'd left her behind?

"I…" She looked up at him. His eyes searched hers. "I'll be here when you get back."

Frédéric nodded and leaned down to kiss her forehead. Then he kissed her on the lips, chastely, carefully, as though she would shatter, a thousand possibilities flickering out in an instant.

Perhaps he did know.

Nora watched the train rumble away into the distance until it turned a bend and was lost to sight. Then she went home and made herself a cup of tea.

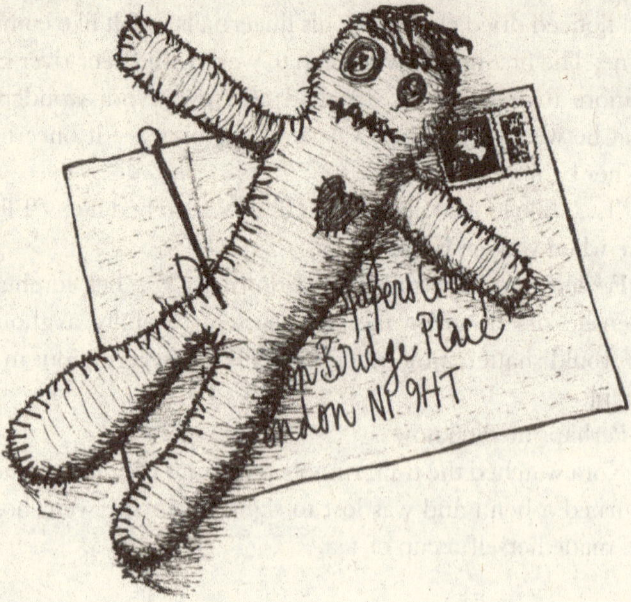
Bridge Place
N1 9HT

Dear Audrey

Dear Audrey,
I've been married to my wife a long time—going on twelve years now! And I love her dearly, but I'm starting to feel like there's no fire anymore. You know that feeling? Like every day is the same as the one before. Now I think I'm starting to feel something for someone else. I don't want to cheat on my wife. What should I do?

Sincerely,
Restless and Confused

Dear Restless,
It sounds like you're writing to me so I can tell you what you already know: if you love your wife, as you say you do, don't throw it away over a moment of weakness. Instead, ask yourself what you can address in your own life to help with that feeling of stagnation. Is work putting too much pressure on you? Take a day off and take your wife to an art gallery. Hell, take a day off and spend it together in bed. Remind yourself of why your love is strong enough to overcome anything.

Sealed with a kiss,
Audrey

Dear Audrey,
I've just started this great new job, and I love all the people there. I've been getting close with one of them, a guy I

work with, and sometimes I feel like he wants more. And he's really, really fit (I mean, for an older man). The problem is, he's married. What should I do?

Warm regards,
Crushing on a Coworker

Dear Crushing,
You don't need me to tell you that getting involved with another woman's husband is bad mojo. How would you feel if he was doing that to you? How will you feel when he does it to you next? If that's not enough, a messy affair could put your career on the line. It's best not to touch this one. Plenty of fish.

Sealed with a kiss,
Audrey

Dear Audrey,
I took your advice and spent the day with my wife. You were right—I'd forgotten how enchanting she can be. It was like we were in our twenties again and the world was still a beautiful place. But while we were out, we actually ran into her—the other her. The woman. Then later, she texted me while my wife was in the shower, and asked me out for coffee. She's clearly into me, and now I don't know what I want. I can't stop thinking about her.

Sincerely,
Confused All Over Again

Dear Confused,
It sounds like you took a really good step with your wife. It was bad timing that your distraction chose that moment to show up, but it doesn't erase what you're lucky enough to come home to every night. An illicit fling might be fun for a few weeks, but it will cause everyone involved a lot of pain for a lot longer. Take my advice and focus on repairing your relationship.

Sealed with a kiss,
Audrey

Dear Audrey,
So, I tried to stay away. I was so relieved when he called in sick. Though that's bad isn't it, being grateful that someone's poorly? Anyway, it doesn't matter, because he *wasn't* sick. I ran into him on my way home coming out of the art gallery with his wife. And we said hi and everything, and it was awkward. She was really nice though.

Anyway, I sent him a text later, just like "glad you're feeling better! :)" and he asked me to meet him for coffee! And I don't know what to do. There's nothing wrong with grabbing coffee with a coworker, is there? But I don't know if it's that kind of coffee, or like…the other kind. The naked kind.

Do I want it to be the naked kind?

Warm regards,
Still Crushing

Dear Audrey,
I know, I know. You're right. You're always right. But I did go for that coffee, because I didn't want to be rude. I mean, I could hardly say "No, I don't like coffee," and then show up to work the next day with java. That would be weird.

She was wearing red. I know, I should have walked away then and there. I told my wife I was running to the bank. Why did I tell her that?

Anyway, we talked for over an hour, and it was so amazing how I could just be myself. I love my wife, but sometimes it feels like I have to filter what I say, you know? Like I can't just relax. But I could with her. So after, I walked her to her front door. And then I walked her upstairs. And then I walked her inside.

I don't know why I'm telling you all this. There isn't really anyone else I can talk to. ~~My friend Brett~~ sorry, I shouldn't really use names. My friend, he would kill for a healthy, stable marriage like mine. He'd gut me if he knew I was throwing it all away.

You're right. Once is enough. I won't see her again. I won't even look at her.

Thanks for listening.

Sincerely,
Repentant

Dear Audrey,
I keep telling myself I'll give him up, but I can't help it. He's been over three times this week. I feel awful, knowing what his wife is going through. Does she know? Is she suffering in silence? Or does she think she married a good man? Part of me wants to tell her, to split him apart and watch her eviscerate him for what he's doing. But then, maybe I'm just as bad. Maybe I'm worse.

There's something else, too. Yesterday, we were upstairs, and he was trying to...you know. Get started. He cried out in the most awful pain. I thought for a second someone had tried to cut off his... well. It was like any time he reached for me he'd experience this horrible agony. I told him he should get it checked out in case he has testicular cancer or an infection or something, but he said no because then he'd have to tell the doctor he'd been here. I still think he should, but there's no arguing with men.

Warm regards,
Guilty Crush

Dear Guilty,
It sounds like it's high time to step off this ride. It's only going to hurt both of you in the end; plus, if there's something wrong with him

down there, have you considered that he might pass it on to you? That you could become ill, or infertile, or worse? You're young and pretty, in a ~~harlot~~ blonde kind of way. You could have anyone else in that office. Step back before you destroy more than you bargained for.

Sealed with a warning,
Audrey

Dear Audrey,
I tried playing it safe, but god, I'm so BORED! All I do is go to work and pretend to care about cross-platform data analysis, and come home, and do it all over again. I'm so sick of my life. Being with her feels like the only time I'm truly awake.

There's a problem, though. I've been having trouble with my…performance. And not even in the normal way—not that I would know. In the way of excruciating pain every time I even think about her.

So, I went home and lay down on the sofa. I've been sleeping there more and more lately. And I was checking my email, but I was still wrung out from before and I dropped my phone. And when I reached over to get it, I found something underneath the sofa.

A doll.

Not a kid's doll. We don't have kids. I mean a hex doll…a poppet, I think they're called. With creepy button eyes. And there was a sewing needle right in its…between its legs. Right there.

Oh man, it was weird looking at that thing. It didn't look anything like me, but I felt like I'd caught my reflection in the mirror. I know that sounds crazy, but listen—I pulled the needle out, and I swear, I *felt* it. I felt it come out. And I had to lie down again. But after, I thought, maybe that's that. So, I went to see—right, no names. I went to see her. But it didn't make any difference. The pain still came.

Audrey, I think my wife's put a curse on me. I don't know what to do.

Sincerely,
Desperate and Scared

Dear Desperate,
A curse can only be lifted by the witch who put it there in the first place. Try to do it yourself and you'll only make it worse.

Your wife obviously knows about your affair. There's nothing you can do but throw yourself on her mercy and apologise.

Beg.

Beg for your pathetic little life. Beg for another chance to spend every single day fighting to be worthy of her. Tell her you love her, and only her, and your harlot was a midlife crisis-induced blip of poor judgement. Remind yourself each night that your place by her side is a gift.

She might forgive you. She might not. But until you try, you'll never touch a woman again.

Sealed with a promise,
Audrey

Dear Audrey,
I thought for a long time about what you said. I do still love my wife. We've both made mistakes. We've both caused each other pain. We've been to hell and back and somehow, she's never given up on me. I broke my marriage vows, and I'll do whatever it takes to put them together again.

She was out doing the shopping when I got in, so I waited in our room. It was messier than I remembered. There were a lot of tissues, and she'd been reading—

one of those mystery novels, and something by someone named Corinne Boyer. I picked up the book, and that's when I saw the letters.

Letters I'd written.

To Audrey.

I'm sorry. I know I screwed up. Please forgive me, Anna.

David

Dear David,
Do you remember when we first met? You told me you'd fallen "under my spell". And it made me laugh, but not for the reason you thought. I laughed because there was no spell. I didn't want one, not for you. I wanted it to be real.

I want to believe it still is. But I don't know. I need time.

I'll remove the curse. If you stay— if I stay—it should be our choice.

No spells, no chains. Just you and me.

Anna

Dear Audrey,
He took me aside at work today and told me he was leaving. Not the company. Leaving me. He said he needs to fix things with her. I mean, I get it. It was nice being wanted, you know? But it was never a forever deal. I hope things work out for them. I just keep telling myself that.

Anyway, thanks. You were right. You probably get that a lot.

Warm regards,
Moving On

Dear Anna,
I'll be waiting.

David

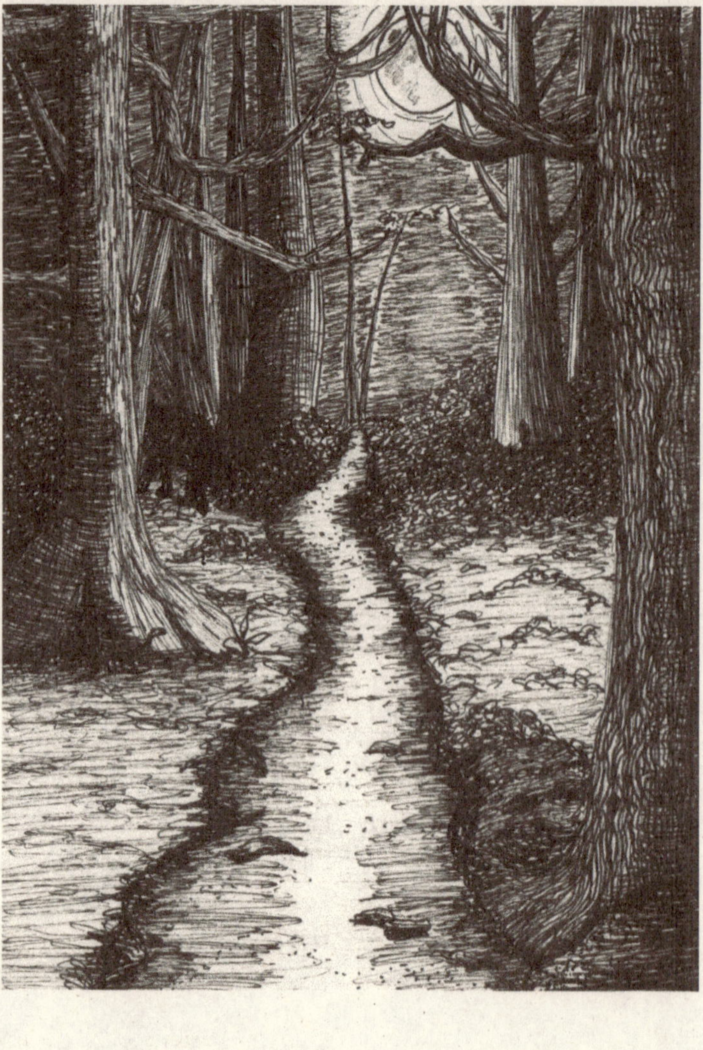

Running with Wolves

R ed's grandmother had three rules:

Beware the dark woods at night.
Don't stray from the path.
Bring extra sandwiches.

Red's mother had many rules: Don't smile at strange men. Keep that red hair tied back when you go into town. Always save a pound for the donation box at church. Wear heels no lower than one inch and no higher than two. Never wear red when the moon is full. Be respectful to your grandmother, but don't indulge her too much. She had so many rules that Red lost track and gave up trying to remember them all.

"She's only watching out for you," said Tobias, as they dangled their feet over the pier into the river below. Red wasn't supposed to get her feet wet. There was a delicious thrill in watching the cool murmurs of the river curl around her toes and imagining her mother's disapproval.

"Well, she should stop it. It's suffocating."

Tobias looked down at his feet. They were bigger than hers. "She wants you to be safe. So, she gives you all these rules that make *her* feel safe. It's all she knows."

Red looked at him crossly, annoyed by her best friend's fathomless patience. "Your family's not like that."

He shrugged. "Sure they are. It's just for them the safe place isn't somewhere you go or don't go or hide away in. It's on the inside. In here." He pointed to his heart.

She scowled. "My mother should invite your family for tea." Immediately she regretted it. Her mother would never invite Tobias' family for tea. Nobody invited Tobias' family for tea.

A shadow flickered behind his eyes. Then he smiled and pointed at the water. "Look! You made a friend."

Red looked down. A tiny minnow curiously nudged her toes. Then, apparently satisfied, it swam away.

She pulled her feet out of the water and let them dry in the sun.

"Are you going to your grandmother's today?"

She nodded. "They're angry again."

"At you?"

"At each other."

"Why?"

"I don't know. My fault, probably." She stood, leaving wet patches on the wood where her feet had been. "I should go. It'll be dark soon." The sun was already casting long, molten shadows across the treetops.

Tobias stood too. "I'll walk with you."

"Sure. Whatever." Red liked it when Tobias walked with her.

The woods near where Red's grandmother lived were new growth, the trees still young and slender. There had been another wood there, a long time ago, and you could still see rotting stumps the size of minivans. Tobias said that now animals built their nests in them, squirrels and badgers and shrews. Tobias knew a lot of things.

They walked along a path worn smooth by generations of footsteps. Bindweed and wild wormwood peeked out between the ferns and briars. They stopped just before Red's grandmother's cottage came into view. Tobias didn't like to get too close to people. Most people. She waved lamely and he smiled before turning away. Red watched him go, trying to pick out the exact moment when Tobias disappeared and all she saw was forest, but she never could.

Red's grandmother was making hawthorn berry tea. Red smelled it as she walked in, the familiar spicy strawberry-cider scent that always clung to her clothes after she left. She kicked off her boots by the door.

Bundles of dried herbs and crow feathers hung in the front hall, bound with twine and red and purple ribbons. Just beyond them hung her grandmother's old red cape, patched and worn to sepia brown with time. Red went into the kitchen and stopped. The old oak table stood in the middle of the room. Her mother was sitting at it.

"Hello, Winnifred," said Red's mother.

Red looked between her mother and her grandmother, who was fussing around the stove. Her grandmother smiled at her, but her shoulders were tight. She poured hawthorn berry tea into three brown mugs. For the first time Red could remember, her grandmother looked very old.

"Hello, dear. Come and warm yourself up. Your mother and I were just talking." She handed Red one of the mugs and took the other two to the table. Red's mother took hers and set it down without drinking it.

Red sat down cautiously.

"Winnifred," her mother said, "I've received a letter. From the municipal board of education."

She tensed, hands around the hot tea, and mentally catalogued all the things she could be in trouble for. The confused, frightened mouse she'd found hiding in the air vent. The letter to her mother which had never made it home. Victoria Cadwell's broken nose.

"She started it," Red said.

Her mother's face went blank. "Who started what?"

Red took a sip of her tea. "What sort of letter?"

"They've offered us a bursary."

Now it was Red's turn to be confused. "What's that?"

"It's like a scholarship. They're giving you a free place at a new school. A better school. In the city."

Red went very still. "What do I need a new school for? I already have one." It was crumbling and small, but she could walk to her grandmother's in less than twenty minutes. If she went to a new one, she'd have to go home with her mother instead. And she couldn't sit by the river with Tobias.

"Yes, darling, but this one would offer you a lot more opportunity. It's respected. Henry Channing-Bryce teaches there!"

"Who?"

"That's what I said," muttered Red's grandmother.

"He—never mind. Winnifred, you're a very lucky girl. You'd even get a room of your own for the whole week!"

"I'd have to *live* there?" she shrieked.

"You'll have possibilities that we never had," Red's mother went on. "Think of everything you'll learn."

"But I learn things here. I learn maths in school, and Grandmother teaches me all the plants, and Tobias—"

She stopped. Her mother narrowed her eyes and took a breath before exchanging a look with her own mother across the table. Red's mother and grandmother didn't always get along, but they had an unspoken language that Red wasn't a part of. It made her angry.

To her horror, it was her grandmother who said, "Maybe it's worth giving it a try, Red. Even for a term. See if you like it."

"But I won't like it." Red fought down the rising panic. Once they started ganging up on her, she knew her time was running out. She stood up and sloshed hawthorn berry tea onto the table. "This is my home."

"A stone cottage in the woods isn't a real home for anybody," her mother said impatiently. Then she flushed and looked over at Red's grandmother. Red saw the flash of hurt in her grandmother's eyes, and she used the moment of distraction to bolt out the door.

Shadows were beginning to fall across the path and weave throughout the lower branches. She knew the woods pretty well, though not as well as her grandmother did. She turned away from the usual road home and didn't even notice when she stumbled off the path.

A flurry of crows took off in the distance. The twilight deepened and midges flew in and out of the fading light like will-o'-the-wisps. Dead leaves crunched beneath her feet.

She stopped and looked up at the treetops. The dead leaves crunched again, and it took Red a moment to realise that the footsteps weren't hers.

Her grandmother's warnings flashed through her mind. She hadn't brought any sandwiches.

Standing a body's length away was a wolf—brown and russet shot through with gold, like sunlight caught in autumn leaves. It looked at her with big amber eyes. She took a step back, heart in her throat. She'd never seen a wolf before.

Red stayed very, very still. She tried to picture in her mind how close her grandmother's cottage was, if they'd hear her if she called out, but she wasn't sure.

The wolf barked at her sharply, making her jump. Then, astonishingly, it turned and trotted away. Red watched it go, waiting for its shape to disappear into the wood before allowing her knees to give out.

She didn't know how long she remained collapsed on the forest floor, watching the shadows grow longer and longer until they devoured the light. Maybe it was only a few minutes, or maybe it was a lot more. She stayed until she heard new footsteps and scrambled unsteadily to her feet. Her legs felt like they hadn't been used in months.

It wasn't a wolf, this time. It was Tobias.

Her mouth dropped open. She wondered if she was hallucinating, like those people in the desert who started to think they saw the ocean. And yet, Tobias didn't look out of place at all. He looked as much a part of the woods as the shadows and the leaves beneath their feet.

"Hey, Red," he said shyly, and any doubts she'd had melted away. Suddenly she felt ridiculous.

"I saw a wolf!" she blurted, because it was all she could think of to say.

"Oh yeah?" He grinned. Red couldn't tell if he believed her or not. He came over and took her hand. "Come on, my house isn't far."

She looked at him in surprise. She'd never been to Tobias' house. She knew he was self-conscious because of the things people said about it. About them.

They walked along narrow, winding badger paths overset with briars. Red didn't know how Tobias could see them. She couldn't see much of anything. It wasn't long before the path grew wider and starlight filtered through the thinning canopy, and they came to a long, low house.

"Back when this was a provincial park, the caretaker lived here. But then the government didn't want to pay him anymore, so he left, and…well…it's not as secluded as it looks, if you walk about ten minutes that way there's a road that connects to the highway." He looked at his feet, and she realised he was stalling.

"It's beautiful," she said. The paint was sunstripped to the colour of unbleached linen, but smoke rose from the chimney and the windows were filled with warm light. Purple foxgloves grew by the door.

Tobias smiled in relief, and they went inside.

Red was greeted with a smell of piney woodsmoke. It reminded her of the Lapsang tea one of her mother's boyfriends used to drink. Unlike her grandmother's cottage, which felt bigger on the inside than it did on the outside, Tobias' house seemed to shrink around them. The wall to one side of the door was taken up by mounds and mounds of coats, and the other wall was filled with mounds and mounds of books.

A young woman met them in the entrance hall. She was taller than Tobias, with chestnut-coloured hair—brown and russet with sparks of blonde, like sunlight caught in autumn leaves. She grinned when she saw them.

"Mum's making something to eat. She figured your friend would be hungry."

Tobias unlaced his boots and placed them carefully by the door. "Great. Red, this is Verity."

Verity waved before stuffing her hands in the back pockets of her jeans. Red knew that Tobias had a sister, but she'd never met her. She waved back shyly.

They followed Verity into the kitchen, where the woodsmoke gave way to smells of simmering herbs and seared meat. Tobias' father sat at an ancient dining table, worn into a mottled landscape of scratches and polished edges and stains left from spilled tea. He was old, maybe as old as Red's grandmother, but he had broad shoulders and muscled arms as taut as tree roots.

Tobias' mother had long, long white hair pulled into a braid that ran all the way down her back. She was stirring a big copper cookpot. When the three of them entered the kitchen, she put down the stirrer and gave Red a warm hug.

Red stiffened. Her mother never hugged. Her grandmother did, though, big lumpy ones that smelled of hawthorn berry tea. Tobias' mother smelled like charred marshmallows.

"Red! How lovely to finally meet you. I hope you weren't out in the woods too long, I know they can be a bit unsettling at times. Are you cold? Here, sit by the stove and warm up. Verity! Phone Red's grandmother. Let them know that she's here safe. Her number's in the book. Tobias, set the table."

Red bit back a smile as Tobias pulled out a stack of shallow bowls and dutifully placed them around the wizened wood. His father slowly got to his feet and filled a cracked pitcher with water.

They sat down to eat and everything tasted of thyme and pepper and forest, and Red wondered what her mother and her grandmother and everybody else in town were so afraid of.

Afterwards, Red offered to help with the washing up.

"Don't be silly," said Tobias' mother. "You are a guest in our home. Tobias and I will do it." She tossed a dishcloth at his head. Red left them and wandered into the sitting room, the one that smelled like Lapsang tea. Tobias' father was tossing a handful of dried cedar leaves onto the fire.

Red hovered in the doorway.

"Cedar is for cleansing," Tobias' father explained, without looking up. "Cleaning out the dinnertime smells, and any anger that's been brewing during the day." The room filled with the smell of soft, sweet greenery.

"I know," said Red. "My grandmother uses it too." After a moment, she added, "I was named after her."

The firelight cast harsh, lupine shadows into the man's face. He nodded like Red had uncovered some deep philosophical truth. "What else does she use?"

"Um." She wondered if it was a trick. "She makes charms out of ribbon and rowan berries and leaves them on the windowsill. To protect us. My mother doesn't like them."

He smiled wryly. "I remember."

Red inched farther into the room. "Did you know her?"

He didn't say anything for a long time. Red wasn't sure if he'd heard her. The fire crackled at his side and the burning logs once again overtook the scent of cedar boughs.

"We're from a forgotten age, your grandmother and I. We outlasted the princes and queens and trolls under the bridges. We were here when they took the wood from us and we were here when it grew back anew." Tobias' father looked at Red for the first time and smiled. "She's adjusted better than I have, I'm afraid. Old habits."

He pushed himself up off the floor, wincing, and settled into one of the oversized armchairs. "I'm trying to start now, with Verity and Tobias. That's why I'm glad he has a friend like you."

Red smiled, then felt a stab of guilt. "I'm going away," she said.

He tilted his head curiously, the way Tobias sometimes did. The firelight tinted his eyes golden.

"My mother wants me to go to a new school. I think it's expensive but I get to go for free. I don't really know how it works." Her words were tumbling out too fast. "Do you know who Henry Channing-Bryce is?"

"Never heard of him."

"Me neither." That panic started to roll through her again, and she bit her lip hard to keep from crying. "I don't want to go," she whispered.

"Surely one school is as good as another. Won't they teach you numbers and geography and Latin and all the rest of it?"

Red didn't know anyone who learned Latin in school, but she didn't say this to Tobias' father. Instead she said, "This is my home."

"Ah." He nestled deeper into his chair. Dishes clattered in the kitchen. "Home is a funny thing. There aren't many animals who bind themselves to beam and stone the way you do. You do that long enough, home becomes nothing more than dust and dead skin held together by memories. It's no way to live." He watched the flames whip in and out of shadow. "The forest folk, they understand that home is something you carry around inside of you. Home is a state of being."

"But..." Red struggled to make sense of this. "I won't be able to see Tobias. I mean, not every day."

"You'll carry him around with you too. Just as he'll carry you. And anyway, that's what those things with all the buttons are for. Like a telephone but it's also a tiny computer."

"Tobias doesn't have a smartphone."

"Ah well, maybe he will soon. Verity's just got herself one. Ridiculous things."

Red allowed herself a small smile.

Tobias appeared in the doorway. He looked between them nervously.

"Do you want to go outside?" he said. "The moon's out."

Red nodded and waved goodbye to the old man. She and Tobias went out and sat on the front steps.

"What were you and my dad talking about?"

"Smartphones," Red replied.

"Verity just got one."

They looked up at the stars, a multitude of glowing silver embers against a charred sky.

"Maybe you'll get one too."

Tobias shrugged. "What for?"

"Just to talk. When I'm away."

"Where are you going?" He said it lightly, like he was expecting her to say Disneyland or Narnia or Kokomo. When she didn't answer, he turned to look at her.

"A new school. One with famous teachers and…rooms and stuff. My mother wants me to go."

Tobias was quiet. A cool wind blew the piney, cedary scent of the forest around them in little whirls.

"How much does a smartphone cost?" he said.

"I don't know. We can split it."

He looked back up at the sky. The moon was so full and bright that its edges bled into the darkness like an oil slick.

"Your father says that home is something you carry around inside you. He says it's a state of being."

Tobias nodded. "He's pretty smart about some things."

Red thought about her grandmother's cottage, with its herb bundles and charms on the windowsill and hawthorn berry tea. "Is there nowhere that feels like home to you?"

He considered this. "The woods, I guess. These woods. I can run in them and discover things and howl for hours and hours. If I want to."

"You really go into the woods and howl at things?" She wasn't sure if he was teasing.

He grinned at her. "When I'm stressed. Or overwhelmed. Or just happy. I think about all the things I'm feeling that are too big for my body, and just…" He leaned his head back and let out a long howl. Red was impressed. He sounded like a real wolf.

"Try it."

She flushed. If her mother could see her! Red tilted her head back and looked up at the stars, sweet and glittering, and howled. It didn't sound like a real wolf. It sounded like a girl.

"Perfect!" he said. "You're a natural."

Red fought back a grin and gave him a gentle shove with her shoulder.

She looked up at the stars again, and the moon guiding their way across the sky. From her house the moon looked cold and distant, but here it seemed friendly and encouraging. She remembered how angry she'd been with her mother, and how scared, and she thought about the new school in the city with Mr Henry Channing-Whatsit, and about her grandmother and Tobias' father and how Tobias would get a smartphone and how she'd teach him to use Instagram. The thought made her giggle, and the giggle rose out of her like champagne bubbles and turned into a long, clear howl. This one was better.

Tobias' voice joined hers and for just a moment she felt so completely, exhilaratingly free. Together, on the dusty step beside the foxglove blooms, they howled side by side to the smiling moon and stars.

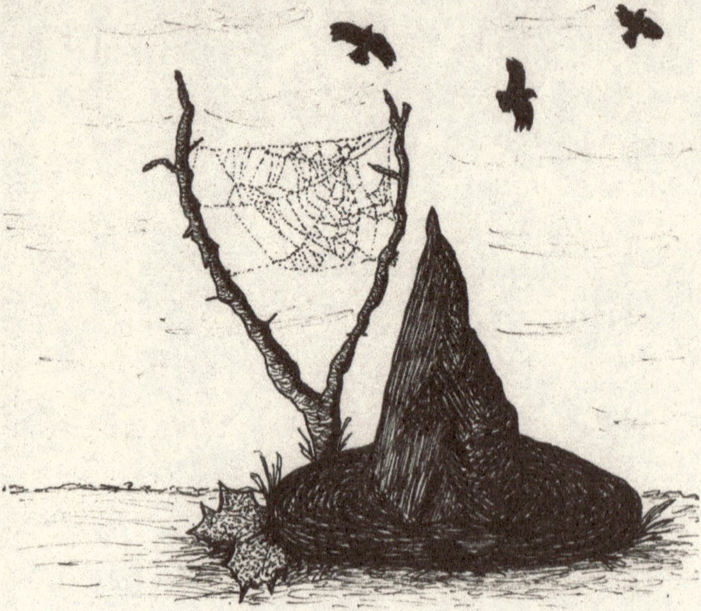

Waking the Witch

"Let's play witches."

It always begins like this. Black pointed hats someone's mum got for two euros in the after-Halloween sales, a whisper of something they don't yet have words for, a thread binding them to ancestors they don't yet know exist. Deep, deep in their blood and bones they know it's not a game, and yet—to play is to create, and they are feeding the growing hunger in the only way they know how.

I can see them under the rowan tree from my kitchen window upstairs. I don't know their names but I've seen their mothers around town, crossing the street to avoid meeting eyes with me and leaving a pastel cloud of heliotrope perfume in their wake. One of the girls—tall for her age, and gawky as a colt—has got hold of a broomstick from somewhere and is waving it around haphazardly, oblivious to the scattering crows. It has a plastic handle and bits of straw poking out of the metal threading.

"*I'm* going to cast a spell on Trevor Cole," says another, and I smile. Of course, even at that age, they understand the deepest power of all. She's more soft-featured than her friend, less like a colt and more like one of the bramble roses that grow by the roadside.

"Good thinking," says the third. This one is beginning to show signs of womanhood in her high cheekbones and aquiline nose. She is a young kestrel staggering on unsteady wings. "For this spell we'll need Eye of Newt—" she plucks a stalk of pineapple weed from the grass—"Frog's Warts…" in her child's imagination, a golden hawksbit blossom becomes an oozing substance of esoteric power. Bramble Rose makes a face.

"And…" Kestrel tilts her head to one side, considering. "Spider's webs."

There.

I remember. It comes in flashes at first, true things scattered like dandelion seeds amidst the games and shallow dreams. She too will remember this, this feeling of a cog slipping gently into place, and she will long for it again and again.

"*Spider's webs?*" The Colt shuffles behind Bramble Rose, who's only about half her size. "Why?"

"To trap a lover," Kestrel says, as though this should be obvious. I wonder if this is the first time she's ever spoken that word; stripped of its complexity, it tumbles easily from her lips.

The girls nod hesitantly, knowing this to be a true thing. They go off in search of an abandoned web and return to the tree before long. Bramble Rose holds the delicate woven silk between two sticks. The hawksbit and pineapple weed have been forgotten.

"Right," says The Colt, who's overcome her trepidation, "what do we say?"

"Does it need to rhyme?" asks Bramble Rose. "They usually do, don't they?"

"I don't think so. I think we just need to use old words and say what we want." Kestrel peers at the web. "Let's say, 'May we hold the adoration of our true loves until this web be torn asunder.'"

"What's 'asunder'?"

"It means 'in a million pieces'. Come on."

The three girls in their pointed hats stand close together, hands joined by two sticks of wood—rowan wood, witch's wood, though it will be years before they know this—and a glistening shimmer of spider's silk. At this age magic is so simple, so uncluttered, as easy as believing in curse-breaking kisses and the watchful whispers of autumn leaves.

The November wind caresses her new daughters, who are just beginning to wake.

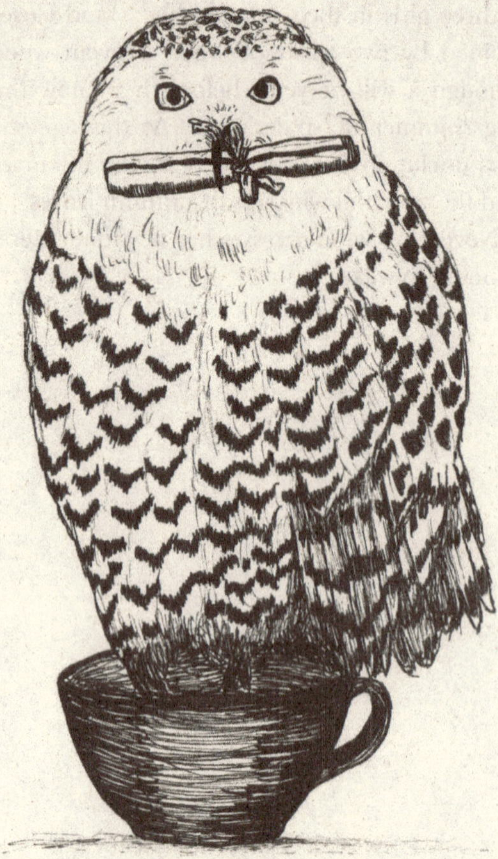

The Road to Faërie

Jillian's sister ran off six years ago with a man who offered her a bowl of pomegranate seeds.

Jillan's sister went to the crossroads six years ago and made a deal with the devil for a pair of wings.

Jillian's sister danced naked in the forest six years ago with a local coven, and pulled the moon right into her being, and nobody's heard from her since.

Or so the rumours said.

The truth was, nobody really knew what happened to Jillian's sister Lily, not even Jillian. All she knew was that on May Eve, two weeks before her graduate thesis was due, Lily O'Connor walked into the woods after a heavy rainfall and didn't come back.

Living in a world without Lily in it felt like walking around with her shoes on the wrong feet. Ever since they were small, right up until Jillian's Incident, they'd been a single cohesive unit: Jill'n'Lil. Like the sisters in *Sense and Sensibility*, or *Goblin Market*.

Jillian was thinking about Lily as she walked into the café at five minutes to nine and pulled on her apron. Last year they'd given her one with the word "Jillien" embroidered right on the front, so she didn't have to wear a plastic name tag anymore.

She ran her finger over the maroon threading with a mixture of pride and disgust.

Dylan was already there when she arrived, running hot water through the coffee machine. His apron had a name tag on it that said "Dylan". He gave her a cheery wave as she walked in.

"Morning," she mumbled. She went over to the coffee machine and filled a teapot with hot water and a sachet of Bewley's Original Blend tea. Then she poured a shot of espresso and added it to the teapot. Dylan stared at her.

"One of those nights, was it?"

"No judgement," Jillian said, as she sipped her tea. She wrinkled her nose and added a glug of honey to the pot.

Dylan knew about Jillian's sister, but he didn't know it was exactly six years to the day. The night before she had pulled out Lily's unfinished thesis, a yellowing manuscript edged in dust, and ran her fingers over the crisp title on the first page.

Fairy Folklore in Popular Culture: A Comparison of Oral Tradition and 21st-Century Myth.

Jillian had wanted to hold it tight to her body and never let go. She'd wanted to tear it in half.

Fortified, she turned to Dylan. "And how's yourself?"

"Yeah, grand, yeah. I've my last exams on Thursday, and then my years of higher education are finally behind me." He said it with his easy smile, but Jillian had seen the dark circles under his eyes, the way he scrambled to finish persuasive essays in between brewing lattes, and knew what a relief it would be for him. She had watched his trajectory with envy and a touch of guilt. After her Incident she took three months off university with every intention of returning, but never did. Instead, she'd worked more hours at the café and watched Lily flourish, her sister's light glowing against her own stagnant darkness, the gap between them growing ever more impassable.

Until the May's Eve when the gap devoured her entire world.

"So, what's next?" she asked. "Now that you're finished?" It was like picking at a scab.

"Find myself a grown-up job, gods willing," he said. She turned so he wouldn't see her face and self-consciously reached for the embroidery on her apron. It was the only anchor to reality she had left, the only thing that said *I am here, I am real*, and it wasn't even spelled properly.

The morning's first customers pulled her from her thoughts, and she forced her attention instead on the rumbling milk steamer and the pervasive scent of freshly ground coffee, the familiar rhythms of the everyday. She let Dylan work the cash register, because he was the one who could be charming before ten a.m.

She was putting a final flourish on her half-hearted latte art when the screams began.

Jillian's head shot up. Coffee cups splattered and chairs screeched throughout the café. From high above them came the beating of wings.

An enormous snowy owl swooped towards her. It landed with a small scuffle and a thud on the countertop. A rolled up piece of paper was caught in its beak.

Jillian stood very still. She was certain that if she moved, it would claw out her eyeballs.

"I think it's your acceptance letter to Hogwarts," Dylan joked, but she noticed he wasn't moving either.

In response, the owl spat the paper at its feet. It stared up at Jillian in what seemed to be a very indignant manner.

"Well, grab it then," Jillian said.

"You grab it."

"I have delicate lady fingers."

The owl gave her a disgusted look, then kicked the paper towards her with one of its clawed feet.

"It's probably someone's pet," Dylan said, relaxing slightly, as Jillian snatched up the roll of paper. It was tied with a yellow ribbon. He and the owl watched as she pulled it loose.

The note was written in ballpoint pen. Lily's loopy, oversized scrawl careened across the page, as though she'd tried to write it in the dark. Jillian forgot how to breathe.

OMG I KNOW I'M SORRY YOU'RE PROBABLY SO ANNOYED WITH ME RN but I just arrived and this place is everything I thought it would be. They're going to let me interview them for my thesis. I only have like a second but I'll definitely, definitely be back before the end of semester.

If you want you can send a reply back with Fred. He'll make sure it gets to me. His name's not really Fred, but I can't pronounce his real name—it's spelled sort of like if you dropped a handful of scrabble tiles and then coughed on them in Norwegian. I'll try write again soon. Don't freak out and please remember to call the helpline if you're ever not okay.

PS—Fred's the owl.

It was dated three days after Lily's disappearance.

She read the note again. Distantly, she heard wings beat against the stale air. Her eyes snapped up, desperately searching the room, but he was already gone.

Abstract:

British and Celtic folklore is experiencing a resurgence across all entertainment mediums including film, television, literature, and comic books[1]. Some of these follow their original source material precisely, while others deviate and add new facets in service of the story and the age in which it is being told. This begs the question: is any one "true" source material more authentic than any other? Does the very nature of the subject matter allow for cultural malleability? Here I will explore recurring patterns across folklorically influenced stories and how they compare to storytelling of the modern day (for detailed examples, see analyses of Emma Bull's *War for the Oaks* and Black and DiTerlizzi's *Spiderwick Chronicles*, appendix B).

Jillian lay in bed in her tiny flat and ran her fingers across the latticework of pale scars that decorated her wrist. It had become a sort of map between past and present, each line a road not taken, a wrong turn, a dead-end regret. Sometimes she felt as though she was looking down at a sprawling cityscape, watching a tiny Jillian run up one scar and down another, trying to find her way home.

Lily's letter lay beside her on the mattress. After the owl flew away and the scattered patrons burst into relieved applause, Jillian had gone into the break room and smashed all the empty Fentimans bottles that were set aside for recycling. Dylan found her sitting on the floor surrounded by shards of broken glass.

He shut down the café and made her a pot of chamomile tea. She hated chamomile tea, but sipped it dutifully because he was being so kind. Her mind settled into a soft, fuzzy calm.

He didn't ask her any questions, for which she felt profoundly grateful. Maybe there was nothing to say.

Now she watched a narrow shaft of moonlight slip across the room, and the hollow silence of night broke in waves against her skin. Her mind flickered in and out of the edges of dreams. When she woke, it was with the touch of owl feathers at her fingertips and the scent of the wildwood fading in the morning light.

There were still hours before she needed to be back at the café for work. She shook off her weariness and went for a walk in the early morning mist, hoping to clear her head. Lily's letter was clenched in her pocket. The air was damp and fresh and heavy with the scent of growing things; an image from her dream fluttered behind her eyes for an instant, then was gone.

Jillian had never been a morning person, even before the Incident, but the soft half-light and the silence—a gentler, kinder silence than the one that came to her at night—made her understand the appeal. She walked to a nearby city park dotted with old-growth trees and empty swing sets and winding paths carpeted in pine needles. It was Lily's favourite place.

After Lily's disappearance there had been inquiries and a half-hearted search that quickly fell by the wayside. After all, there was nothing to suggest she hadn't left of her own accord. One of the officers told Jillian it wasn't unusual at that time of year, students crumbling under the pressure of term drawing to a close. She'd turn up when she was ready. Guiltily, Jillian had realised she found that more horrifying than the gruesome images she fell asleep with at night—the idea that Lily could have simply left her, walked away when she needed her most.

She drank in the crisp, cool air and glanced up to see a white owl swoop low overhead. Her breath caught.

The owl landed on a cedar branch and folded its wings against its sides. It blinked down at her. Jillian followed until she stood at the base of the tree.

"Hello?" she called. Then, hoping no one was listening, she said, "Fred?" She couldn't tell if it was the same owl or not.

Morning sun was starting to break through the treetops, sending curtains of light tumbling to the leaf-strewn floor. The owl hooted at her—at least, in her general direction—and then rose from the bough in a flurry of feathers. It stretched its wings and turned its body on an angle, one wing pointed down and the other skyward. It seemed, impossibly, to fly *into* one of the curtains of light. By some trick of light and shadow, it vanished between one moment and the next.

Jillian looked around, trying to pick out where it had gone. Her exhaustion mingled with a rising sense of panic and loss. The sun climbed higher, and the lingering shadows dissolved into morning.

※

The concept of time as it relates to Faërie is one that appears to fall in and out of fashion in literature. In early folkloric tradition, time was believed to move differently in Otherworlds than it does in the world we know. We see this recurring idea in the Celtic myth of Oisin and Niamh, the folk tale of Rip Van Winkle, and

The Chronicles of Narnia, among others. There is no consistent calculation to determine time spent in one place or another, though in the Cornish legend of the Woodsman and the Well[9], three days in Faërie passed as six years in the man's home village (see Aarne-Thompson-Uther Index #729).

More modern stories of the supernatural, however, generally eschew this unwritten tenet—*Stardust*, for example, illustrates clearly defined borders between one world and another without any discrepancies in the passage of time. This may be part of a larger cultural shift that seeks to convey the two worlds as more symbiotically and interdependently intertwined.

Jillian prepared a pot of Bewley's Original Blend and added two shots of espresso. Dylan handed her the honey.

"Do you want to talk about it?" he asked, after she'd taken a restorative sip.

About what, she almost said, then hated herself. But she didn't know what to say, where to begin. There was so much loss all tangled up together, so many roads to what could have been eroded and decayed beyond recognition. So many pieces of herself sloughed away by the ache of time.

"When we were little," she said finally, "there was this wood behind where we lived. It wasn't huge or anything, but you know, when you're that age…" She glanced at Dylan. He nodded encouragingly. "And we had this game where we would search for doors to fairyland. We'd look under logs and in the crevasses of trees and stuff. And once…once, Lily disappeared for two hours. I went out of my mind. After, she didn't even realise she'd been gone."

Jillian watched foamy bubbles meander over the surface of her concoction. She was suddenly struck anew by how truly disgusting it was.

Dylan poured himself a shot of espresso. "Did the note say where she was?"

They're going to let me interview them for my thesis.

Jillian shook her head. "No. I'm not sure she…when she left, the police asked us if she had a secret boyfriend or something. But there wasn't anything like that. She would have told me." The last words, for reasons she didn't quite understand, tasted like a lie.

"You think she left, then?"

She blinked, startled. "I mean, when she disappeared. We don't know what happened." But her own voice had already betrayed her. Of course she'd left. Lily had left her. Maybe she'd always known.

Someone knocked at the café door. It was ten minutes past nine. Jillian and Dylan ignored them.

"Was this when that started?" Dylan said gently, and nodded towards her wrist.

Jillian's other hand went to it automatically, the touch repulsive and comforting at the same time. "No," she said. "No, that was earlier. I went through a bad breakup with my fiancé, and I didn't I didn't handle it very well."

"I'm sorry." He sipped his espresso, eyes downward. "I didn't know you were engaged."

She shrugged. "Another life." Another road not taken. After he left her—saying it was too fast, too much, too hard—the world around her seemed to speed up while everything inside her slowed down. She'd fall asleep for an hour and find she'd walked through entire days without noticing. Tearing herself open was the only thing that made time stand still, just for a moment, as she watched all her mistakes blur in streaks of red across her skin. Until the night it got really, *really* bad and she was taken to hospital for assessment. She ended up staying for three months.

"She was all I had left." Jillian gripped her teacup hard enough to turn her knuckles white. "Why didn't she...why didn't she *say* anything? Why didn't she at least tell me where she was going? Why...?" She bit back the question she really wanted to ask, the only one that really mattered.

Why didn't she take me with her?

"I don't know why," Dylan said, even though she hadn't really been asking him. "We don't always see what people are going through on the inside. But I know that sometimes we're given chances and only one shot at them. Maybe she didn't have time to tell you. Or maybe..." He hesitated. "Maybe she just needed to make her own path."

His words settled into her stomach. After the Incident, Lily had become sister, mother, therapist, friend, always on call in case Jillian got scared, always ready to tell her she would be okay. Deep down, Jillian knew it wasn't fair to put all of her pain on her sister, but that only made her hate herself more. She hated that she couldn't be strong and brave on her own, that Lily always had to be the one keeping her together.

She was holding her back.

Jillian drained the last of her tea and went to open the café door.

who may have partly inspired Spenser's *Faerie Queene*. Other examples include the ballad of Tam Lin, variants of Beauty and the Beast, Rossetti's *Goblin Market*, and the 1986 film *Labyrinth*.

If you reach back far enough, each of these story archetypes[16] have one essential element in common: free will. No mortal can be taken by Faërie without their consent.

To understand the perenniality of this seemingly counterintuitive idea, we must look to why we tell these stories in the first place. Are they intended to be cautionary tales for wayward daughters? Or reminders that we are the architects of our own fates? Perhaps the wolf in the dark woods was never a monster to be feared, but an invitation to reach for one's own agency and sexuality—maybe for the first time. (See Aarne-Thompson-Uther Index #333; evolutionary analysis in appendix C.)

The ink was beginning to smudge on the letter, already worn down by too many readings. Jillian wondered if one day it would disappear entirely. She sat on her bed with the letter on one side and her apron, brought home for washing, on the other.

and this place is everything I thought it would be
I'll definitely be back before the end of semester
Don't freak out and please remember
everything I thought it would be
before the end of semester

please remember
everything

Maybe Lily still believed she'd be back in time to finish her thesis. Or maybe she left it behind, left everything behind, for a chance—her only chance—to fly.

The maroon threading glistened up at her. *Jillien.* Dylan would never get an apron with his name sewn onto it, she knew. He would grow wings and fly away just like Lily flew away, both of them spiralling ever upward into the endless open world.

She could feel it happening again, time speeding up around her as everything inside her ground to a halt. Dylan getting his diploma and leaving the café. Someone new taking his place. The world shifting and sprawling out in all directions without her.

Her wrist began to itch with dozens of bloody memories. And suddenly Jillian felt a wave of exhaustion, followed by fury. She was so, so *sick* of it, of being the one always left behind. Of being someone's responsibility, someone's problem. For the first time in almost seven years, Jillian's bones ached to fly too.

She pulled a pair of scissors from her bedside table and, before she really understood what she was doing, began to pull the maroon threads apart. They snapped one at a time, rough and ragged, like a gaping wound that grew wider with each messy snip. And with every thread that broke free, time moved a little bit slower.

When she was finished, the embroidery that was once her name was a riot of chaotic red thread. She stared down at it as if she'd never seen it before. It looked like something left behind from another life.

Time stood still.

She remembered what Dylan had said, about being given chances and only one shot to take them. Maybe that was her problem—she'd spent so long waiting for a chance to be handed to her that she'd forgotten how to build them herself. She'd forgotten that they were within reach every single day.

She carefully folded Lily's letter, and then she folded her apron, and put them both in a drawer. Then she lay down and began to dream about what the future might bring.

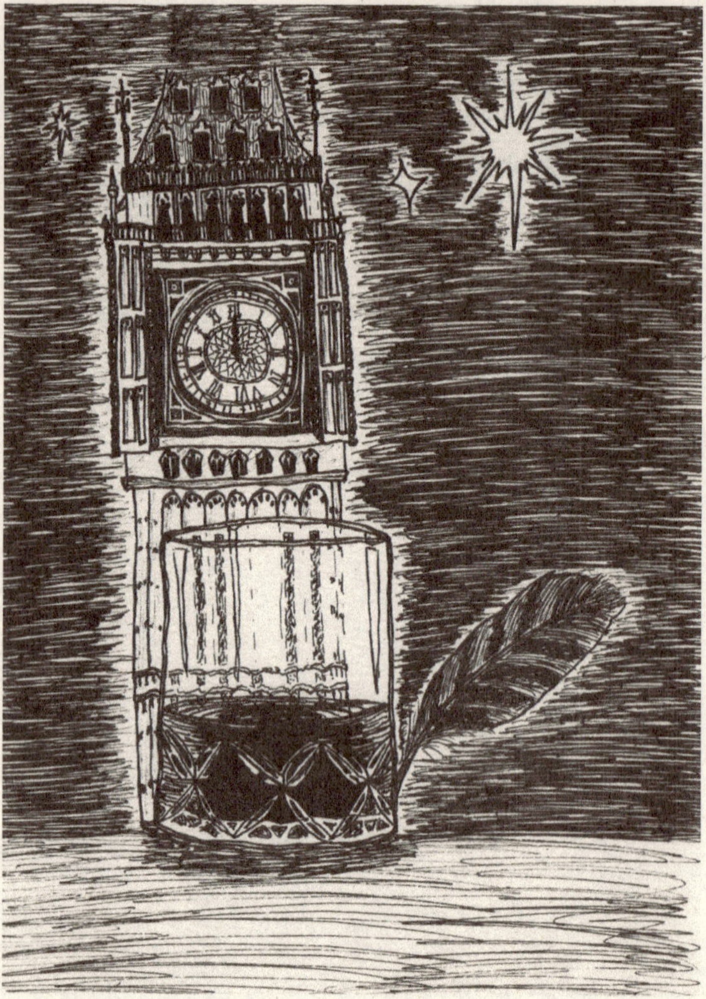

Lost Men

Michael became a veterinarian.

He was good at it. Always kind and compassionate, even in the face of senseless death. When he wasn't too overworked, he also ran a small toy hospital where children could take their dolls and teddy bears for a checkup. Michael would listen to their heartbeats with a stethoscope, and say *hmmm...*, and prescribe the poor patient a lolly—"but make sure he brushes his teeth!"

Wendy became a librarian. She was good at it, too, especially the story circles she held for young children. When her American beau, Malcolm, said he didn't want a wife who worked, Wendy left her paid position and stayed on as a volunteer. Malcolm couldn't quite decide whether or not he'd won.

John became a drunk. He wasn't very good at it.

After they returned to the grey, unforgiving London streets, John and Wendy carried Neverland cached away inside of them, holding it close like a precious secret only they could share. Michael forgot quickly, of course, as very young children do, the wonders of one pretend game dimming against the light of countless others. By unspoken agreement, John and Wendy's memories existed in silence—in shared glances and soft, dreamy smiles. John often fell asleep with the ache of longing clutching at his throat, and woke tasting a fading dream of sea salt on his lips.

It helped to know there was one person who understood, even as their childhood wonder became more perilously fragile. He and Wendy were so close in age that they often knew what the other was thinking. Sometimes they joked that they took turns being the eldest. Very soon they'd both be thirteen, and thirteen, as everyone knew, was the beginning of the end.

Sometimes, when neither of them could sleep, John would lie down beside Wendy and they'd remember Neverland together without saying a word.

But when there were bad days, when their parents began arguing late at night when the children were supposed to be asleep, the time Michael got really ill and the doctor stayed all night, John and Wendy would grip their hands together, and John would whisper, "Second star to the right."

And Wendy would say, "And straight on 'til morning."

As they got older, Wendy's body began to soften and John felt strange lying beside her in her bed, so instead he sat on the floor and leaned his head back against the mattress. John was changing too, though he couldn't see it; often Wendy's friends from school would come home with her and try to catch his eye. One of them kissed him in the garden. She tasted mostly of emptiness, with a faint whisper of that smoggy, metallic London taste. It was nothing like the wood-smoked breath of the untamed Indian princess who'd once kissed him at the edge of the lagoon, a lifetime ago.

The girl did not come back.

Wendy met Malcolm at one of their parents' charity functions. He was in London preparing to open the first European branch of his father's hotel chain. Malcolm smoked only the very best cigars and left them, half finished, smouldering in their ashtray. John didn't like him. Michael didn't like him either, but said their job wasn't to like him, it was to keep him in line and make sure he made Wendy happy. John wondered when it had become Michael's turn to be the eldest.

John poured himself a glass of his father's whisky. He didn't like that very much either.

The day Wendy and Malcolm announced their engagement, their family had a small soirée at Claridge's Hotel—"Let's throw the poor fellas a bone," Malcolm said, "we'll be putting them out of business soon enough."—and Wendy and John found themselves side by side out on the balcony. The city sprawled in all directions beneath them, and the night sky, dimmed by the lights below, glittered determinedly. John picked out the north star.

"Second star to the right," he whispered. His voice sounded funny in his ears. How many glasses had he drunk? Not so many, surely.

Wendy wore a blue satin dress and her hair up in a complex knot. She looked like their mother.

The night air made him bold. "Do you reckon he ever thinks of us?" John asked.

"Who?" said Wendy. But it wasn't a real question. Of course she knew. The boy who never grew up meant more to her than to any of them.

But then she turned to look at John with blank eyes the colour of her dress, and the warmth leached from his body.

"Peter," he said.

They hadn't spoken his name in twelve years.

A tiny frown creased her forehead. "Was he one of Father's friends?"

"I…" John gripped the railing for support.

She smiled gently. Wendy did everything gently. "I should get back to Malcolm. He doesn't like waiting."

She turned and went back inside. John watched her go. Then he went to get another drink.

Malcolm's hotel, the Star Regent, opened the weekend a travelling fair came to Kensington. The streets teemed with Londoners and others, strange visitors from far-off places, humming with debaucherous possibility.

The hotel had eighty-seven rooms, and a restaurant, and a ballroom, and Malcolm invited all the Darling family to stay for the grand opening. John's room was small, but had a tiny balcony with a view of the fair below. The balcony was built of decorative wrought iron, so John could look down at his feet and see snippets of people walking to and fro seven storeys beneath him.

Michael had a room across the hall. He knocked on John's door to tell him they were all meeting at the restaurant to celebrate, the Darlings and Malcolm's parents all the way from New York. John said he just needed to have a wash and then he'd join them.

Michael gave him a hard, suspicious look. John would have felt insulted if his brother hadn't known him so well.

He did get as far as washing and combing his unruly hair into something resembling the hair of an international hotelier's brother-in-law. Then he stepped back onto the balcony and looked down at the glittering lights of the fair. He wondered how many children would become Lost that night.

He took the lift down, feeling slightly nauseous. He'd been in a lift only twice in his life, and he wasn't sure he trusted them. As he emerged, gentle strains of piano keys fluttered out of the restaurant. John stopped just outside the entrance and peeked in.

Malcolm was holding court at the head of a long table. Wendy sat at one arm and a severe, sharp-nosed woman, presumably his mother, sat at his other. Mrs Darling looked enchanted. Wendy looked bored.

John hesitated only a moment, then turned away and walked out the front door.

The park across the street had been transformed into a riot of garish wonder. Stalls selling all manner of worldly bric-a-brac lined the walks, and the air filled with smoke and spices from far-off lands. Electric lights filtered through coloured film made John feel as though he were walking through a crystal prism.

Beyond the stalls, tents of dark velvet proclaimed things like *Cower in fear from the real-life Wolf Man! Exclusive public appearance*, and *See Lahkmet the Snake Charmer, all the way from Darkest Egypt!*

In the kaleidoscopic lights and shadows, it was easy to push away his guilt at leaving the party behind. He didn't want to sit across from his parents, between a brother and sister who were turning into his parents, and watch them all slip effortlessly into a world that was leaving him further and further behind. Here he could shed the past twelve years like a wearisome coat and nobody would look at him twice.

The fair brought people of all shapes and colours—men with charcoal skin, orientals dressed in beautiful silks, gossiping women with kohl-lined eyes and scarves around their faces and hair. Whether they came from parts of London John had never seen, or somewhere far across the sea, he didn't know. As he explored, he passed a woman with coppery skin and feathers in her long, black hair, and a shock of recognition lanced through him. He spun on the spot, trying to hold onto her face in the crowd.

As soon as she was gone, he felt like kicking himself. He was so desperately homesick for something never his to begin with that he was creating ghosts from his own imagination.

He wandered through the crowd, taking turns at random. The lights and sounds made him dizzy. His head ached for something to drink.

He was about to give up and go back to the hotel when he passed a tent that said *See your future with Laughing Water, great Ojibway medicine woman from the untamed wilds of America!* Mottled grey smoke rose from a hole in the tent's roof.

John wasn't at all sure he wanted to know his future. The way things were going, he'd probably be cast out of his family as an embarrassment. Looking around at the fair, he remembered the way he and Wendy used to talk about running away to join a travelling circus, back when Michael was only a baby. Wendy was going to be an elephant rider, and John a knife thrower.

He wondered what his family would think if he simply never came home.

The air outside the tent smelled of evergreen boughs and, strangely, the ocean air. John lifted the flap and went inside.

The only light came from a fire contained in a cast iron pot. A woman sat cross-legged on the opposite side, the one with the feathers in her hair that he'd passed outside. His lungs clenched. She looked so much like her—Great Big Little Panther's daughter, with the dark almond eyes that warmed his dreams on cold nights under the stars. A long time ago.

But then the woman looked up, and John saw his own recognition reflected back at him.

"John," she whispered. It was half question, half answer, and the world seemed to tilt beneath his feet. He'd finally gone mad.

When he didn't move, she looked away. "I am sorry. For a moment, I thought—"

"No," John said, finding his voice. "No, it's me." He crossed the dusty floor and stumbled into a sitting position by the fire. They stared at each other in the dim light. He drank in her features like a dying man.

Tiger Lily spoke first. "I looked for you. You and Wendy, when I came to London. I looked in every face I passed in the street. I thought maybe you had travelled elsewhere."

John shook his head. "I'm here. In Bloomsbury. Wendy might go to America, though." He remembered the sign out front. "'Laughing Water'?"

She smiled sadly. "They chose it for me, the men who own the fair. It is a good life. I am fed, and left alone. Mostly." She turned her gaze back to the fire. "When my father died, I was to become chieftess. But there was still so much world I had not seen, so much beyond Neverland, so Peter brought me here. He told me he would come back for me in seven days. Then I would return to lead our people."

With a sinking feeling, John realised he knew this story. "He didn't come, did he?"

Tiger Lily shook her head. Her brave resolve wavered. "I learned that people here look at each other with suspicion when their skin is…not like yours." She met his eyes, so much paler than her own. "I found work here, telling fortunes, speaking the words of my people, though they call it Ojibway. Here my skin, my face, becomes a story."

"Can you really see the future?"

She shrugged. "Some. Pieces, in the smoke. The rest I make up. No, your husband has no mistress. Yes, she will return to your bed. Your sons will grow to be brave and strong." She grinned, and for a brief moment she was the wild Indian girl John remembered. He blushed.

"Would you like me to see for you?" Tiger Lily asked.

John tore his eyes from her and stared into the flames. It was so different from the roaring hearth fires they had at home. This was a wilder, more primal thing that made him think of long nights in the treetops, of air heavy with sea salt and pixie dust.

"No, thank you."

John stepped into the dark lobby of the hotel. The tables had been cleared of dinnertime debris; there was no sign that the Darlings had ever been. The quiet felt surreal after the luminescent chaos of the world outside.

He stepped behind the empty bar and poured himself a glass of whisky. There wasn't any ice, but that was alright. He set the glass down on the countertop, went back around to the other side, and pulled out a stool. Then he sipped his whisky alone in the dark.

Another stool slid out beside him.

John didn't look up. Instead he stood, went around the bar, and poured a second glass.

"Wendy missed you at dinner," said Michael.

John sat down again and stared into his drink. "I'll apologise in the morning." It felt like his life was one big apology.

Michael picked up his glass. "I've decided to go into veterinary practice."

"You'll be excellent," John said, and meant it. Michael had the gift of making a room feel calmer just by walking into it.

They sat in silence for a moment. John was happy for him, but he couldn't hold back the crushing feeling that both of them, Michael and Wendy, were drifting slowly and steadily away.

He lifted the whisky to his lips, willing it to burn away his insides, to burn away the whole world.

"Second star to the right," he muttered, and drained what was left in his glass.

Michael sighed and lifted his too. "And straight on 'til morning," he whispered.

John choked on his whisky.

He swivelled in his seat to stare at his little brother, ignoring the splatter of liquor on his shirt. "But…" he sputtered, "you didn't remember. After we came back, you forgot. You forgot everything. You were only a child."

Michael took a sip, then set the glass down and pushed it away. "I didn't forget," he said. "Never. I chose. We all did, by agreeing to come back to London. We chose to grow up."

I didn't, John thought miserably. Growing up never felt like a choice. It was something that just sort of happened to him, infected him, like a contagion of the spirit.

He looked down at his glass and was disappointed to find it empty. Loath as he was to admit it, Michael was right. He could have stayed with the Lost Boys, fighting pirates and singing around campfires for all of eternity, but he'd chosen to return. They'd chosen to return as a family.

Michael might have read his mind, because he said, "Do you ever wish you hadn't?"

"Every day," John replied, surprising even himself. "Do you?"

His brother considered this. "I don't think so. I think even then a part of me understood that children can't really, *really* become world explorers and pilots and lion tamers and all the rest of it. Imagination didn't feel like enough anymore. I wanted to see the world for real."

John nodded. Michael was what their father called an "old soul". Maybe he'd been grown up on the inside all along.

Michael gently took the empty glass from his hands. "There's a lot of world out there, John."

He thought of Tiger Lily, paraded like a trophy for the hungry eyes of English men, whose world had become smaller than she could ever have imagined. He had roads open to him that she never would. He was lucky.

They left the bar and took the lift back upstairs, turning to go to their separate rooms. John didn't sleep. Instead, he sat down on the soft carpet behind the balcony doors and waited for the new day to break the sky apart.

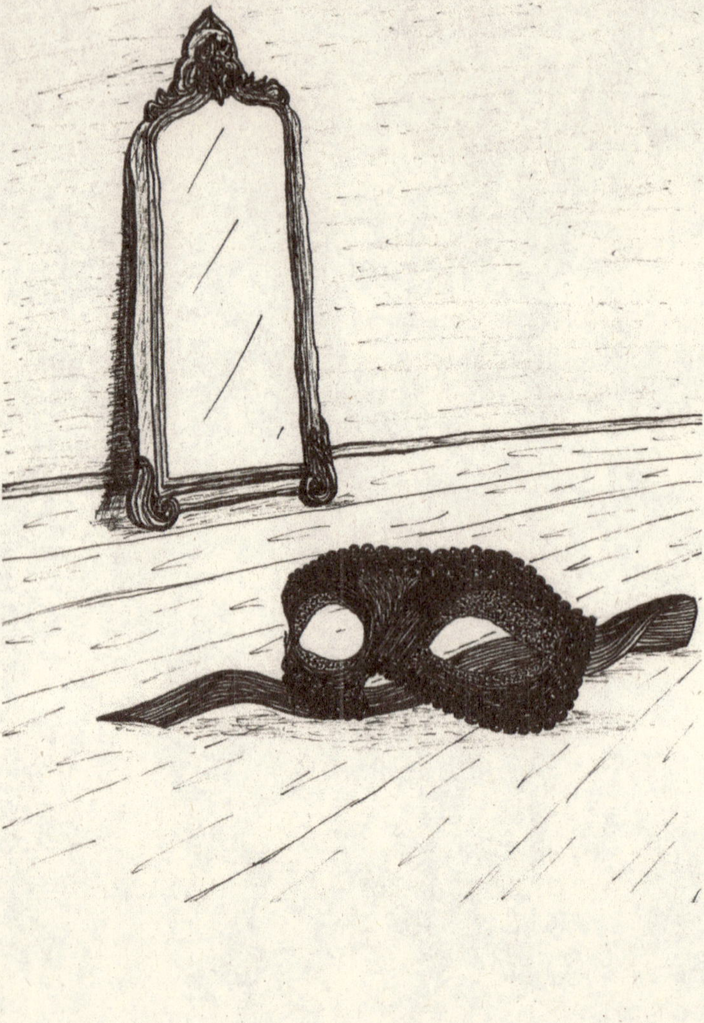

An Ephemeral Quality

My earliest memories are of thread.

For hours I would sit on the floor of my mother's atelier collecting the cuttings that lay discarded throughout the workshop, picking up each one and inspecting it carefully between pudgy little fingers. Purple ones were my favourite. Whenever I found one I would put it in the pocket of my dress for safekeeping. It didn't matter that she would have given me all the purple thread I wanted, if I'd asked; it was a treasure hunt of my very own, and I collected tiny victories like pebbles on a beach.

Even then I understood that my mother's work was very special. The busiest times were near Halloween, of course, and just before the Winter Solstice Parade. I watched as she transformed boring old people into sorcerers, mermaids, tree spirits, jungle queens. Under my mother's touch her clients grew tall and proud and wise. They *became*, until the costume wasn't a costume at all.

On our last day in that town, the one in the south of England where I was born, the workshop floor was covered in threads the colour of autumn leaves—vivid reds and golds and dusty browns. It was just before the Solstice Parade. The woman who stood in the centre of the fitting platform was dark-skinned and gold-edged, and my mother had dressed her in the gown and matching headdress of a firebird. The headdress was made up of golden feathers and it came down over her face in swirls of red and gold leather. I could only just see her eyes. They looked like deep pools of hot chocolate. When she moved the feathers rustled like the crackling of a campfire.

The firebird woman looked so powerful and brave that I was a little afraid of her. Not my mother, though—she wasn't afraid of anything, not even when smoke started to rise from the fabric where she touched the dress. I picked up the delicate threads from the floor, all the different reds and oranges and golds together, and then hid while my mother finished.

The costume shop was always cold because the heating was always broken, but that day it got too hot too quickly. I thought my mother started to look a little worried, but that couldn't be right. She was probably just excited to go see the parade with me.

The woman handed my mother some money. Her hand left charred black streaks on the wooden door on her way out. After she was gone my mother played with the rings on her fingers and said maybe we should stay home that night.

Later there was a fire at the parade, a big one. It was in the papers the next morning; three people died, including a girl only a little older than me. Mother told me we needed to pack quickly. I could still smell smoke on the air as the bus took us away.

The phone rings. I stare at it warily before taking it from its cradle on the overcrowded desk.

"Harlan Atelier," I say.
"Hello, is this Eleanor?"
"No, madam, this is—"
"I'm looking for Eleanor Harlan Atelier."
I take a breath. "This is Eleanor Harlan's Atelier, but—"
"Great. Put me on the phone with her."

My fingers tighten against the bakelite phone. "I'm afraid she's not here, Mrs…" The voice sounds vaguely familiar, but it could be any one of several malnourished Louboutin-shod housewives.

"When do you expect her? It's very important."

There's a clock ticking on the wall. When this place was alive with movement I never noticed it, but now each passing second rings out like a gavel.

"She won't be coming back," I say. "She's dead."

The first time I said those words out loud I felt dirty inside, like I'd made a racist comment or made fun of someone for being in a wheelchair. Now, though, I've said them so many times that they've lost all meaning. *Sorry, my mum's not here. She's gone out for lunch. She's having a cigarette. She's dead.*

"Oh." The phone is silent. "Who are you?"
"Ezrabet. Her daughter."
"The scrappy one?"
"There's just the one, madam."

The woman sighs with all the restraint of a southern screen starlet. "She was letting out the waist on a dress for me. I need it by Friday."

I remember what my therapist said about controlling my anger, and I imagine a soft curtain coming down as I breathe deeply.

"Your name, please?"

"Dawn Woodruff."

I put the receiver down on the desk. My arm aches from holding it. I locate Dawn Woodruff's heinously sequinned cry for help on the rack of completed alterations.

"Your dress is ready, madam. You can come and pick it up any time this week."

After I hang up, I go back to my scattered piles of forms, notes, and administrative jobs-in-progress, shoving down my annoyance and my jet lag. I'm numb and exhausted but I keep signing, printing, scanning, tallying numbers because watching one column of figures flicker by after another is easier than what I'll have to do next: go through her things. Unpack her life.

The bell over the door jingles. I tell myself again that I'll take it down, knowing that I won't until the entire place is in boxes. I stifle a groan and look up.

A man is standing in the doorway—my mum's age, maybe, maybe a little younger. I can't tell. He looks like one of those airport-novel fantasies of a sexy librarian, gold-rimmed glasses and messy mousey hair touched with grey, and smelling of coffee and vanilla aftershave. I glare at him suspiciously.

"Hi. Sorry, hello. I was hoping you could help me with something."

"I'm sorry, sir, we're not taking any new clients at the moment. In fact, we're going to be closing permanently." But he's already digging into his ridiculous leather man-purse. His glasses slip down his nose and he pushes them up with one hand.

"Yes, of course, sorry, I'll only be a moment." Before I can say anything else he pulls something black and compact out of his bag. He holds it out to me.

An Ephemeral Quality

It's not what I expected.

The fabric is so dark that at first I think it's velvet, but it turns out to be soft-brushed leather. The shape is simple, but elegant—sweeping lines around almond-shaped cutouts for the eyes, tilted up at the corners. A slight pull in the fabric at each side suggests laughter. A thick satin ribbon extends from one side.

"I have the other one," he says, as I take the mask from him. He digs around in his man-purse again and pulls out a matching satin ribbon. "It came apart a while ago. I've had it a long time though, it held up pretty well."

I hold the mask carefully and run my thumb over the leather. There's something startlingly intimate about the motion. The piece is well crafted, the stitching strong but unobtrusive. I turn it over in my hands and whatever Sexy Librarian is yammering about dies in my ears.

It's one of hers.

My mother's signature is in the corner along the bottom seam, glistening in silver ink. It doesn't seem like her style—unadorned, almost utilitarian—but it's the same signature as the one on the dance costume she made me when I was five. She stopped making costumes not long after that, directing her talent instead to hemming tattered Levis and graduation dresses.

"Sure. I'll fix it," I hear myself say. My voice sounds like it's coming from underwater.

"Great!" The man beams like a puppy. He looks around the workshop. "I heard about Eleanor."

The world comes back with a roar.

"There will be a funeral. I don't know when yet. There's a mailing list." I point to the clipboard hanging from a hook beside the door. Then I toss the mask onto the table. The man winces.

"Right. So can I come and pick up the mask tomorrow, maybe?"

"Sure. Tomorrow's fine." My words are all hard edges and right angles. I go back to the pile of papers and scan the top one. I read it three times and still have no idea what it says.

"Thanks." He shifts awkwardly. "I guess I'll see you, Ezrabet."

He pulls open the door and disappears into the street. The bell has fallen silent by the time it occurs to me to wonder how he knew my name.

※

I let myself into my mother's apartment, where I'm staying while in town. I try not to spend a lot of time there; it feels like one of those reconstructionist museums, or a moment frozen in time. My mum's antique sewing machine is still there, the one she learned on before buying a more efficient one for the shop. Its black curves and gold motifs make it look like a vintage Cadillac among tractors. The walls smell like cigarettes and there's food in the kitchen slowly sailing past its use-by date. A strip of police tape clings to the door frame.

I can't handle sleeping in my mum's room or my old one, so I sleep on the sofa in the living room. It's more threadbare than I remembered. The mirror against the wall is the same though, a great gilded baroque thing that she picked up at a rubbish market when I was twelve. I remember thinking that the mirror and the sewing machine should run off together, leaving behind the rest of this trailer trash hole.

I know I should eat something but my stomach's still turned from jet lag, so instead I make a pot of tea and empty my bag onto the kitchen counter. The black mask tumbles out of the debris. It looks even darker here in the dim lighting. I find some stray needles and thread in a kitchen drawer and begin reattaching the ribbon to the little lining strip.

My mother could have done it better, but when I'm finished it doesn't look too bad and holds securely. I run my finger over the silver signature. It feels like something left behind from another life—a time when she was an artist who saw so much beauty in the world, before she started drinking, before she started running from something deep inside herself. A time when we were happy.

The leather is cool against my fingers and again I'm struck by that inviting sense of intimacy, that warm seductive promise. I remember, for the first time in years, the flutter of a firebird's dress. Sooty streaks on the doorframe. The smell of ashes in the air.

I go to the mirror and hold the mask up against my face. My straw-coloured hair escapes around the edges and stubborn freckles spill across my nose. When I was young I was convinced that one day I'd grow into a great beauty like her. It never happened.

The satin ribbons are smooth and weightless. I pull them behind my head and knot them together. The mask slips a little and I tug it back so I can see properly.

The world looks the same. In the mirror, my head tilts curiously to one side and the creases at the eyes suggest an amusing secret. My hair is darker, somehow, and healthier, and I can't see my freckles anymore. I lift a hand to my face and it's only when I see the slender seamstress's fingers that I realise I'm looking at my mother.

I rip off the mask. It catches on my hair, washed out and cracking at the ends, and my stupid freckles are stark against the sudden flush. Maybe I need a proper meal after all.

The mask sits in my hand—simple, unadorned leather kissed in silver ink. I glance uneasily at the mirror once more before shoving the mask back into my handbag.

⁂

Being in the workshop is easier than being in the apartment. The street outside hums reassuringly and the tension in my chest settles down patiently into the waiting room of my brain.

Dawn Woodruff picks up her dress and gets snippy when I don't fold it properly. She makes me glad I left this suffocating country behind. I long for my bright apartment in Chicago—it's an absolute matchbox with only a double hob to cook on, but the windows are tall and look out over Millenium Park. It made the world seem so full of possibility. Once.

The bell over the door chimes.

The man with the purse walks in, glancing around the chaotic atelier. It's taking on the feel of a gutted animal; thin white clothes racks stand empty amidst raw bare patches and the carnage of stray cuttings. He steps around a half-full cardboard box and picks his way to the desk.

"Hey, Ezrabet," he says, and my eyes narrow. Yesterday I'd never seen this man before in my life.

"I didn't tell you my name," I say.

"Right." He tugs awkwardly on his bag. "Sorry, I should have…I'm Brady. I was friends with your mum."

I'm not convinced. "My mother doesn't have friends." Not for a long time. If she did she wouldn't have died alone on a bathroom floor. The thought hits me so hard that I gasp for breath. I cover it with a cough.

"It's been a while," he admits. He studies my face for a moment, and it makes me want to slap him. "Do you have the…is it ready?"

"What?"

"The mask."

It's sitting in my bag under the desk. I want to throw it at him and tell him to get out of my shop. I want to tell him that he's a liar, because if he was really my mother's friend he would have been there. I want him to leave and never come back.

But I also want to see her again.

"Not yet. Tomorrow." I wonder if he knows I'm lying. "I've been busy."

"Of course." He pushes his glasses up the bridge of his nose. "Are you busy now?"

I look at him questioningly. The truth is I'd kill to get out of this room, but I'm not going to tell him that.

"I hear the place across the street has good coffee. Do you want to go sit down for a while and talk?"

"We don't have anything to talk about." I can hear the bitterness in my voice and I hate myself for it. I wonder how long I've been like this.

He sighs. "Oh Ezrabet…"

"What do you want?" I spit the words out like chicken bones. "What are you doing here?"

"I miss her." He says it in a rush. Then he shrugs and pushes his glasses up again. "I never got to say goodbye."

This time I study his face. His temples are going grey and there are lines around his eyes, but he looks like a lost little boy. He tugs on his bag strap and begins to turn away.

I sigh long and hard and force my teeth to unclench.

"I never got to say goodbye either."

The café across the road is typical of the upscale trash I see all over Chicago—exposed Edison bulbs shedding watery light on empty shipping crates that probably cost a fortune on Etsy. I manoeuvre between university students to a table while Brady waits in line. The chairs are mismatched skeletons of wood and flannel upholstery. I settle into one and before long he returns with a black coffee for me and something with cream and sprinkles for himself.

I look at the concoction distastefully. "What in the nine hells is that?"

"It's a…caramel soy mochachino." He bites down a grin.

"That's disgusting."

"Hush and drink your tar."

I take a sip. It's hot and violently bitter. I hope he goes to the bathroom soon so I can put some sugar in it.

"So," he says, "how long are you staying?"

I shrug noncommittally and drink my tar. "Don't know. Not long. I have to get back to work."

"Oh? What are you doing?"

"I work for a dance company."

"You're dancing?" His eyes light up with excitement, and something almost like pride. I want to ask him what on earth he has to be so happy about.

"No, I'm an admin assistant."

"Oh." He looks down at his drink.

The familiar rush of shame digs into my spine. No, I didn't make it. No, I wasn't good enough. "It's fine, though. I get free tickets and stuff." I shrug again. The other shoulder this time. It's hot in here.

"Well, that's good." He sips his drink. It leaves a line of cream on his lip and he wipes it off with the back of his hand.

"Were you really friends with my mum?"

A little smile flickers across his face. "For a long time. We met when we were six and she…she…punched a bully in the face for me." He flushes and hides behind his obnoxious drink.

I take another sip of my coffee. It's horrible. "Do you need to go to the bathroom or anything?"

"Huh?"

"Never mind. So, what happened?"

"We got into a fight. After the, um, the Solstice Parade." He doesn't meet my eyes. "I kept track of her over the years, made sure both of you were okay. I thought about reaching out after you went to Chicago, but it didn't seem like the right time. Then, well…" He pushes back his glasses. "I guess there's never really a right time."

"Maybe if you had she'd be alive right now." The words come out before I can stop them. His face cracks just before he turns away.

"You think I don't know that?" he says quietly.

I want to say I'm sorry. I want to say I didn't mean it, that I'm the one who should have been there. I don't say any of those things. I stand and pick up my bag, the one with the mask at the bottom.

"Thanks for the coffee," I say, and push my way through the tables, hoping that if I run fast enough I can outrun myself.

⌘

When I get back to the apartment, the cardboard boxes I ordered are leaning up against the doorframe. I haul them inside in two armfuls and set them against the living room wall. They stare at me accusingly.

I stall by making a cup of tea. Then I go to the hall closet and pull down boxes of old junk that she left behind. The closet smells like her.

There's a clunky black Polaroid camera, the kind that was big in the '80s and '90s. Some design template books, and a newspaper cutout from the town we lived in when I was a kid. I'm in it—a grainy, pudgy baby in my mother's arms. She's smiling. Her dark hair goes down past her waist. Behind us is the shopfront of her first place, the one that sold the beautiful costumes. The article's headline is *Unlikely Artisan Finds Niche Market in Small Town*.

I set the article aside. Underneath is a tattered flyer in burgundy and gold.

UNMASKED
Samhain Night Masquerade Ball
Come as you truly are!
Sophia Loren Cultural Centre, 31st October, 1989, 7pm

Below the words is a drawing of a masquerade mask made of oak leaves. Roses heavy with thorns climb up the edges.

An Ephemeral Quality

Come as you truly are. I wonder how many people danced in my mother's creations that night. There's a photo, too, faded and scuffed with time and neglect. My mum's in it, maybe my age, wearing a white masquerade mask. Someone's got their arm around her. I peer closer and realise it's Brady—except this version of Brady is a stone-cold fox. His mask is black. They look happy.

I dig around in the boxes some more. There's a surprising number of shoes, T-straps and button-up Victorian boots and Marilyn pumps. An elaborate fur coat, and guiltily I think of the harsh winters in Chicago. While rummaging around, I get stabbed by a stray sewing needle more than once. My finger leaves a smear of blood on the cardboard.

A ribbon pokes out of the chaos. It's thick satin and snowy white. I pull on it, but it's caught on something deeper in the box. I tug gently, shifting the refuse around with my other hand until it comes loose.

Dangling at the end of the ribbon is a white mask.

I stare at it for a moment, watching it spin, then carefully free the ribbon on the other side. At first glance it looks like a twin to the black, but they're not quite the same. This leather is slick, rather than the soft brushed fabric of the black one, and the corners of the eyes are smooth. Instead the leather pulls gently in between them, contrasting the amusement of the black mask with its own faint hint of tragedy. I turn it over and see the familiar signature in silver ink. For a moment I'm tempted to lift it to my face, but a sudden, inexplicable fear catches at me like a bramble thorn. I set it aside instead.

Standing sentry over the mess of junk, the mirror glitters from the second-hand sun off the building next door. The gold around the edges takes on a melted, ephemeral quality. I fish the black mask out of my bag and another guilty flush creeps up as I remember Brady's face, the pain in his eyes. Then I step over to the mirror.

What I see is wholly uninspiring: eyes red from exhaustion, unwashed clothes that have long since lost any prestige, their labels frayed by time and abuse. They look too big for me, like I've shrunk inside them since arriving. The mask hums in my fingers.

I lift it to my eyes.

Seeing her isn't jarring, like I thought it might be. It's like stepping into sunlight. The mother in the mirror appraises me curiously. She looks healthier than I've seen her in a long time. I wonder what she must think of me, her arrogant wayward failure of a daughter.

"I tried," I whisper. "I tried to become someone you could be proud of." As I say it I realise that's part of the story, but not all of it. I went to Chicago because I was running away from what we'd become, from the silence that clung like something rotting and long forgotten. From looking into her eyes and never knowing how much of her was truly awake.

This version of her is different, though. She looks like the strong, confident woman from the costume shop, the one I'd watched pin scarlet feathers to a golden gown so long ago.

I reach out and meet her fingertips in the mirror—long, elegant fingers that always seemed to hold so much poetry. Only the thinnest membrane of glass lies in between.

"Why did you leave me?"

You left. For a heartstopping moment, the words seem to be coming from her. Then I realise they came from my own thoughts, the ones I try so hard to push down. *You left. You went to Chicago and left her all alone when you* knew *she was ill.*

I stare at my mother's wide eyes in the mirror. I see fear in them, and a buried memory bubbles up: a flippant comment at nine years old; being shoved hard against a wall so fast that I didn't know it was happening until my head smacked against the plaster. It's one of the memories I fought to keep buried, but this time I notice something different, something new— the shock in her eyes, and the fear. She was as surprised as I was.

I remember, now, her releasing me quickly and running away. I remember wondering what she was running from.

"You should have told me. You should have asked for help. I would have come back." But even as I say it, I wonder if it's true.

My mother says nothing.

"You pushed me away. You push everyone away." The familiar anger flares up. Its claws reach for my throat, equal parts painful and seductive. "You could have tried to get better. You could have got real help instead of finding it at the bottom of a bottle." The venom in my voice startles me.

Still she says nothing, just watches with that half-smile around her eyes. I step closer. Our noses are almost touching.

"You took the coward's way out."

You left. You weren't there. You abandoned her.

The anger is roaring like a hungry dragon and I try to imagine the curtain coming down, like my therapist says, but it's timid and insubstantial. The dragon waves it away like mist.

"Why don't you say something?" I ask. My mother lifts her chin proudly and defiance flickers behind the mask. "What does it matter now, anyway? You're gone and you're never coming back, you'll never have to look at the screwed-up waste of space you left behind…" I am horrified to find that I'm crying. My voice breaks and the leather grows sticky against my skin.

"Say something!" I slam my hand against the glass. Her hand meets mine, like a high five. Like she thinks it's all a joke. "Tell me how much I disappointed you." I'm so angry that my vision is turning white. "Tell me that I wasn't able to save you." *You should have been there.* I'm having trouble forming words now, and I don't know whether it's from the lump in my throat or the fury or both. I can't see straight. I slam my hand against the glass again. It rattles violently.

"You left me all alone!"

Once more and, in the space between one heartbeat and another, the mirror shatters. I tear off the mask and sink to the ground, sobbing in shame and terror amidst the broken glass.

Brady and I sit in the coffee house. It was my idea this time. He has one of those absurd candy bar drinks and I've ordered a mocha. I glare at him with steely eyes, daring him to say anything.

"Thank you for fixing this," he says, when I hand him the mask. "It's nice to…to have something of her."

"Sure," I say. The white one sits between us on the table. I'm not sure why I brought it. Because of that photo, I guess, that one of him and my mum. "The masks…" I hesitate, uncertain how to phrase my question. But he understands.

"The black one," he says, "makes others see you as you want to be seen."

I stare at him. "No it doesn't."

He shrugs wearily. "It wasn't intentional. I don't think it ever was, really. It's something that just sort of…came out of her. I was having a hard time with…I didn't have a lot of confidence back then, and she was trying to help."

"But—" I stop, fighting the truth, trying not to look at it too closely.

"Why? What did you see?"

I meet his eyes, and his expression softens. He knows. This doesn't aggravate me the way I expected it to.

"And the white?"

"The white shows you as you truly are." He smiles self-consciously. "I was never brave enough to wear it."

I sip my mocha. It's not bad. We sit in silence for a minute.

"I'm going back to Chicago at the end of the week." I don't know what that's supposed to mean to him. We've just met.

After a moment he says, "Okay."

"The coffee's better there."

He doesn't say anything.

"I could give you my email. If you want. I mean, if you ever need to talk or something."

He looks up and a moment of joy flashes in his eyes, like the sun peeking out from behind the clouds. He looks like the guy in the photo then, the one who was so happy just to be near her. I want to ask what happened between them but I figure maybe he'll tell me one day, in his own time.

I pick up the white mask. Once again I'm pricked by that bramble thorn of trepidation, but I shrug it off. I lift it to my face and tie the ribbons behind my head.

Brady searches my face. Looking for her, maybe. I lean forward onto my hand and tilt my chin up, voguing to hide my nerves. Putting on the mask feels like taking something off, like stripping down a layer of skin. I'm about to remove it when he nods, once, in satisfaction.

"You're stronger than her," he says. "You'll be okay."

I smile and undo the ribbon. "You too, you know." I put the mask down on the table and notice, at the join where the ribbon meets the leather, a loose white thread. It slips out from underneath a stitch. I tuck it into my pocket—a tiny victory, like a pebble on a beach.

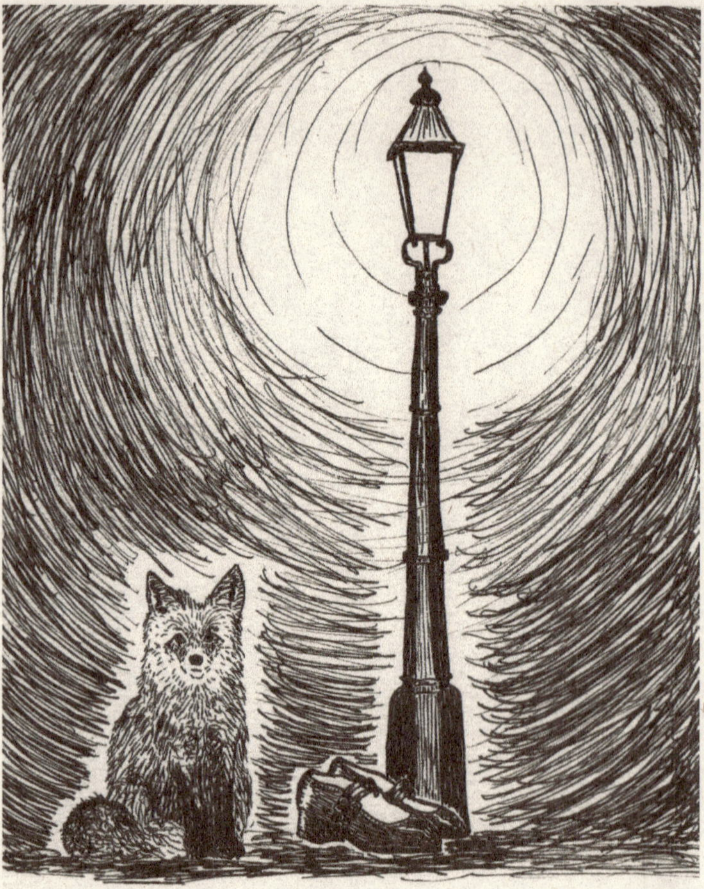

Fox Song

When Addy was very small, her grandmother would sometimes tell her about the time she met a fox person on her way home from work. This was just after the war, when there weren't enough men to go around and women were filling up the men's jobs. Addy's grandmother worked in the copy room of a newspaper, so she said, but she could never remember what the newspaper had been called. It didn't matter, she would say with a wave of her mottled old hand, it was gone now anyway.

Of course, she wasn't called Grandmother back then, or even Mrs Winfell. She was called Betty.

Betty had just spent her very first pay packet on a pair of utterly impractical red patent Mary Janes, and she was pleased as a sack of watermelons (this part changed with the telling; sometimes she was pleased as a basket of figs, or a carton of plums, but she was always pleased with herself). She was admiring them in the evening lamplight, so she wasn't watching where she was going. The shoes went clip, clip, clip against the pavement.

Everything else was silent.

Betty's mother didn't like that she came home alone at night. She didn't argue too fiercely about her daughter taking on work, since they could use the extra money now Betty's father had gone, but she fretted about her out there in the dark.

"The streets are full of toughs," her mother said.

Betty reminded her mother that all the toughs had been knocked off in the war.

"Well, why can't Stanley take you home?"

Stanley Winfell was Addy's grandfather.

He wasn't Addy's grandfather back then, though, and he wasn't a tough, either. He was a busboy at the fancy hotel in town. Stanley assured Betty's mother that he was well on his way to becoming a real chef.

"Because, Mother," said Betty, as she had so many times already, "Stan works even later than I do. He can't leave until everybody's done eating and drinking martinis and all that."

Betty's mother knew this, but she couldn't help worrying.

"He better not be coming home at all hours once you're married," was all she said.

So Betty walked home from the newspaper office in the dark, and her red shoes went clip, clip, clip along the pavement.

They glowed awfully nicely in the streetlight. It gave them a kind of burnt sunsetty colour. Betty looked up as she crossed an empty street and realised, quite suddenly, that she had gone too far. She'd missed her turn.

And the shadows growing longer by the minute, Addy's grandmother would say, while Addy covered her eyes in glee and peeked out through her fingertips.

She was sure she couldn't have gone as far as all that, so she retraced her steps and kept a sharp eye out for her street. Voices drifted through the night air, but she didn't think anything of it until three men turned a corner. They looked up and met her eyes.

Three great, hulking toughs, big as trees, the lot of them. At this point in the story, she'd make her eyes go big and menacing, as if she wasn't a creaky old woman with gaps in her teeth.

They weren't as big as trees, not really, though they did hulk a little—that is to say, they shuffled in the heavy sort of way that men did sometimes when they'd had too much to drink. She was always careful not to tell Addy about the men's hands. Two of them were missing fingers on their lefts; one was missing everything below his wrist. Betty had heard stories about men like that, men who'd done horrible things to themselves and then lied to get honourably discharged so they wouldn't have to fight. She'd never met one.

Now three of them were watching her under the lamplight.

"Look, gents," said the one with the missing hand. "A bird out past bedtime."

Betty held her back very straight.

"What kind of bird do you think it is?"

The men hulked up the sidewalk. Betty debated running. It would be like running from a pack of dogs, she knew; if she tried to flee, they'd hunt her down. It was pure instinct. It was only a question of if she'd be fast enough.

"My money's on a yellow warbler," said another. He had a long scar that cut through one eyebrow and skimmed the corner of his eye. "Look at that pretty hair."

Betty self-consciously touched her golden curls, and the men laughed as if she'd just told them a hilarious joke. Her face grew hot.

"No," said the man with one hand, "she's a robin. Only she's wearing her feathers on her feet."

The others looked down at Betty's shoes. She tucked one foot uselessly behind her ankle.

"Let me pass," she said sharply. "My husband's waiting for me just around the corner."

At that moment, a russet blur darted across the sidewalk between them. All four of them jumped back.

A white-tipped tail disappeared into the bushes.

She should have made a run for it then, Betty realised. But she'd missed her chance, and their attention was on her again in an instant.

"How about this," said the one-handed man. "We'll leave you to go home and pleasure your husband"—his friends snickered behind him—"if you give us those tap shoes as a souvenir."

She couldn't help it. She looked down at her feet. "What on earth for?" The man was hardly going to fit in them.

He grinned and took a step closer. "Something to remember you by."

If he tried to take her shoes, she'd break his nose.

Betty tried not to step back, knowing it would only make it worse, but her feet stumbled backwards anyway. He didn't care about the shoes, of course. They'd probably end up in a rubbish bin somewhere. All he cared about was power.

"What's the matter, Birdie? You scared?"

Betty gave them her most scornful look. "You're one to talk about being scared. Or maybe you'd like to tell me how you lost those fingers of yours."

She knew it was a mistake the moment the words left her mouth. The laughter dissipated in a heartbeat, and maybe some of the drunkenness, too.

"You mind your mouth," he said.

"You did it to yourself, didn't you?" The words kept tumbling out. Maybe she was about to get a beating or worse, but she damn well wasn't going to let these men see her afraid. "Or maybe you couldn't even do that much. I bet you were too scared. I bet you all did it to each other."

Then she heard a sharp, metallic snick. She knew what it was even as her brain refused to process, even as she refused to look.

"For that," he said, holding up a pocket knife, "I'm taking the shoes. And the feet too."

Betty went faint with fear. She wondered what her mother would say. She wondered if Stan would miss her.

Nobody was quite sure what happened next.

The man dropped his knife with a clatter and swatted at his back, shouting incoherently. It took Betty a moment to realise that something had attached itself to the man, something russet with a white tip on its tail.

For a moment, all Betty could do was stare at the one-handed man and the fox digging its teeth into his neck. The other men stared too. Then she remembered the knife on the pavement. All at once, the three of them started towards it, but Betty was fastest and she kicked it hard enough to send it skittering across the street. She shoved the man closest to her with both hands. He stumbled backwards, astonished.

The men hesitated, looking between their struggling friend and Betty's wild eyes. Then they took off into the night.

The fox finally released the man and landed at Betty's side with a hiss. The two of them stared him down until he ran away after his friends.

Betty and the fox looked at each other.

And then, she'd lean in as she got to Addy's favourite part, *all of a sudden, the fox became the most beautiful princess. With long red hair all the way down her back.* And her granddaughter would snuggle in deeper. *And the fox princess walked me home so I didn't have to be afraid.* But foxes didn't like to come inside, so once Betty arrived safely at the door to her mother's house, the fox princess disappeared into the darkness.

Then she'd tuck Addy into bed, and kiss her forehead, and click off the nightlight. Sometimes she'd sit on the bedside in the dark for a few minutes and wonder if Addy dreamed of a fox princess of her own.

But the truth was, it didn't happen quite like that.

She didn't tell Addy that she wasn't all that sure she really wanted to marry Stanley, even if he did become a chef in the end. But times were changing, her mother warned, and there were so few men left, and nobody knew what the future would bring.

She didn't tell Addy that after the two toughs ran off into the night, the first man collapsed onto the pavement with his neck and throat all washed in red, except for a flash of white where the tip of his bone crested the gaping wound.

Most of all, she didn't tell her granddaughter that the fox woman made her feel a shock of longing for something she didn't understand.

Watching the fox become a woman was like watching fresh spring rain—so faint and delicate you were never quite certain where it ended or when it began. A woman stood before her where a fox had been, but the moment of becoming somehow slipped by and was lost.

The woman reached out and gently smoothed the hair out of Betty's eyes. "Are you alright?" she asked.

Betty opened her mouth, then closed it. She looked at the dead man with the blood pooling around his head. It came to her quite suddenly that his blood was the exact same red as her shoes, and then she began to laugh, shrilly and hysterically, with great gobby tears running down her face, even though there was nothing funny about it at all.

The fox woman put her arms around her, and Betty leaned into her shoulder and had a good cry. The woman smelled like garden soil and smoke.

After that, the two of them walked through the darkened streets together. That part had been true. The fox woman pulled a dressing gown off a silent washing line and wrapped it around her bare skin. As they walked, the fox woman asked Betty questions—to keep her mind off the dead man, she supposed. So Betty told her about her job at the newspaper, and about her mother, who meant well but perhaps meant well a little too often, and, haltingly, about Stan. The fox woman told her that she had four sisters, one of whom had just moved to New York and joined a chorus line, and wore fox skin no longer. But she wrote from time to time.

When they reached Betty's house, Betty looked away and pretended not to notice.

The air was warm, and they walked until the paved roads faded into dirt ones, and then they turned off the road and into a copse of old copper beeches and oaks. They sat down in a mossy clearing where they could see stars glittering through the gaps in the treetops. Starlight caught in the fox woman's eyes and reflected back at the sky.

When the fox woman kissed her, Betty felt a jolt of shame and fear, and then something else, something new—a feeling of shedding something she'd spent her whole life suffocating in. She had allowed Stan to kiss her once, and his lips had been scratchy with stubble and tasted very faintly of gin. The fox woman's lips were smooth as chocolate and tasted of the night air.

Kissing Stan hadn't been unpleasant, but kissing the fox woman was like drinking stars.

Later, they lay on the moss and Betty curled the woman's red hair around her fingers. The constellations above them had shifted. The sky was lightening, and it brought a chill against her bare legs. The fox woman reached up and kissed Betty's fingertips one by one.

When Betty returned to the main road, the world looked oddly thin—as though all the houses had been replaced with cardboard imitations overnight. She slowly made her way back to her door. The only sound was the clip, clip, clip of her red shoes against the grey dawn.

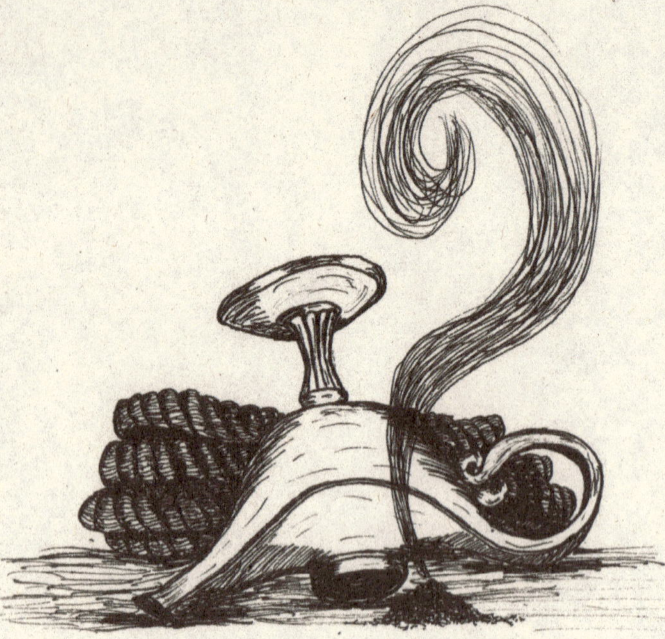

Last Wish

The genie must have been three times the size of my garage, yet somehow fit inside its walls. The room filled with a smell of incense and hot metal. Looking at him was like trying to remember a dream—at one moment distinct, the next a series of loosely connected impressions, sensations, that hovered just at the edge of consciousness.

"I am the genie of the lamp," he thundered, in a voice like old sandstone. "What business have you with me?" The walls shuddered. I glanced nervously towards the house, where my wife was fast asleep.

"Er…yes. You grant wishes, is that right?"

"Three wishes," he thundered, in a voice like winter rain. "But be warned this: for every action you create, an equal reaction will be released into the world."

"Heh?"

"Speak. Your wish is my command."

I struggled to think. The air in the garage was hot and stale and thick. I wished there was a window so I could breathe.

I don't know if I said it out loud or not. Maybe I did. The genie bowed his head low and said, "So it shall be."

The walls rippled. On one side a shimmer sharpened and coalesced until it became a glass pane looking out onto the side lawn. On the opposite wall, the door back into the house flickered out of existence.

"Where's the door?"

"For every action, an equal reaction will be released into the world. For one door to open, another must close."

Right. I shuffled uneasily in my slippers. I needed to get to it then, before I wasted any more wishes.

"Speak your second wish."

I took a deep breath. "My daughter."

The genie raised one heavy, ashy eyebrow.

"My daughter, Lydia. She was…she was…there was an accident. Last year. I wish for her to come back the way she was, alive and whole." The words felt like sandpaper in my throat.

The genie bowed his head. "So it shall be. She will be returned with the rising of the sun."

I stared at him. Could it really be true? I thought of the months I'd spent searching for something—anything—that could bring her back. Anything to take my wife's pain away. Even going as far as believing in the impossible. A swell of discordant joy roiled inside me.

And yet. Nothing was given for free.

"What about that equal reaction thing?"

The genie nodded. "Your child will be returned with the rising of the sun," he said, and I thought I saw something like pity in his eyes, "but you will not be here to see it."

An equal reaction will be released into the world.

A life for a life.

"Speak," he said, more softly, "your third wish."

I didn't have a third wish. I hadn't thought any farther than getting my family back, the three of us. The room that had seemed so stuffy a minute ago was suddenly cold.

"It is not my place to say," the genie said, and hesitated. It made him look smaller, more human, somehow. "But with one wish more you could stay. Leave her to the world of dreaming and live your years as you were intended."

I looked back towards the house, where my wife was tossing and turning to dreams of the daughter she had lost. Of all the years they never got to have together. And I thought of our own, the beautiful memories we had made. The day we were married. The day our daughter was born.

"My third wish," I said. My voice was hoarse.

"Yes?"

"I wish for her to grow up healthy and strong."

He bowed his head. "So it shall be."

All the tension went from my shoulders. There was more of it than I'd realised. It had built up in slow, sedimentary layers since the accident, calcifying in order to hold up even more with every passing day.

I'd got what I came for, yet something itched at the edge of my mind. There would be a price; I'd seen that. There would always be a price.

"And in return?" I asked.

The genie closed his eyes in silence, as though listening. I listened too. The night was still.

"Your garden will wither," he said, in a voice like dying embers. "The soil will turn black with decay, and nothing will ever flourish there again. But your daughter will find love and belonging wherever she goes until the end of her days."

I nodded. It was a fair trade.

The genie vanished somewhere between one moment and the next. The lamp lay discarded on the dusty floor.

I climbed out of the little window and went inside to say goodbye.

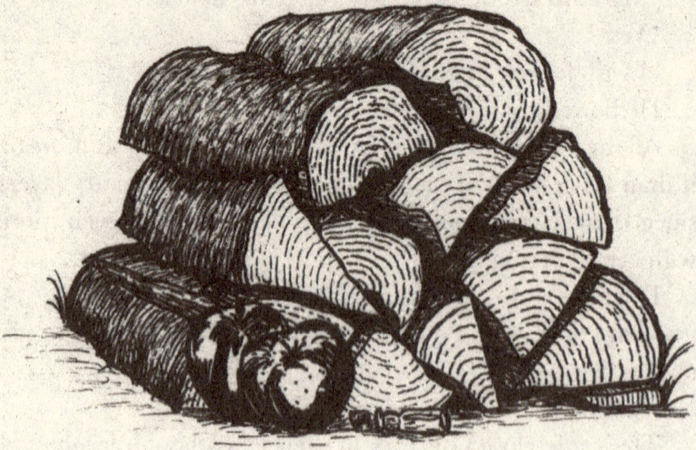

September Sunsets

To summon a lover:

First you need your roses, given by one love
to another, given by moonlight
and sweet goodbyes;
Graveyard dirt (not any grave,
but that you would your lover be:
tinker, tailor, soldier, king);
Some mandrake root, if you can find it;
Ashes from a midsummer's fire;
Briar thorns—those are for loyalty.

And blood.
Of course.

Mix, mix, mix. In silence or in song.
Bind it with bee's wax and spider's webs.
Bind it with promises.
With the striking of a match—
and he will come with the rising of the sun.

Chapter I

She only bought it as a joke, really. The woman at the farmers' market in the next stall over was telling her about her great-grandmother's famous recipe for apple tarts—"pre-dinner" apple tarts with cheese and fresh thyme and prosciutto, and she was asking Emily which apples she would recommend, Pink Lady or Gravenstein or Jonagold, and Emily suggested maybe she try two varieties and mix them together, something sunny and something rosy, and they got to talking. Emily told her how hard things had been since her daughter went off to university, and the woman said maybe Emily needed someone to keep her company, a good man, or woman, if she preferred that sort of thing. Emily said she'd been thinking about getting a cat.

The woman in the stall over sold handmade perfumes, mostly, and a few other things—salves for cuts and bruises, apothecary jars of hawthorn berry cordial, charms to keep the sparrows out of your strawberry patch. So when she pressed the little linen bag into Emily's hand, Emily just thought, *oh well, it might be fun. We've got to support our neighbours.*

The woman bought three Jonagolds and two Bramleys, and a bottle of Emily's special apple syrup.

Chapter II

Emily's cottage stood at the top of the hill at the foot of a sprawling orchard, mostly apples with one knobbly pear tree that Max's parents had bought by mistake. She'd wanted to move to the city when they were first married, but Max was adamant about taking over his family's land, and over time she'd come to love it too. After Jane was born, Max set up a rope swing under the oldest apple tree. But then Max had gone and died, and Jane had gone to school in Edinburgh, and Emily was left rattling around under the apple trees like poor Catherine Linton on the moors.

She built up a little fire in the wood stove, sat on the wine-stained carpet in the living room, and opened the linen bag. Almost everything was already included: a red rose head, brittle and carefully preserved; a stubby beeswax candle that smelled like church; five glass vials. One of the vials said, *Mandrake Root*. It was full of woody bits. Another said, *Midsummer Ashes*. It was filled with weightless grey filaments. *Briar Thorns. Spider's Webs. Graveyard Dirt. Not Included*.

Emily unfolded the instructions. They were written by hand on the back of an Amazon shipping receipt. Roses, the untidy scrawl explained, were for desire. Mandrake was for devotion, midsummer's ashes for joy, and spider's webs to catch and bind. And graveyard dirt, *that you would your lover be*. She was supposed to get it herself.

Emily sighed and put everything back in the bag. Then she threw the bag in the back of a drawer.

Chapter III

"I've been thinking of getting a cat," Emily announced. She was watching the late-September sunset over the apple trees. It was moments like this one that made her understand why Max loved the place so much.

"That's great, Mum," said Jane. She sounded distracted.

"Are you distracted?" Emily said.

"No, of course not. My flatmate was just saying something. A cat is a great idea. Especially as you've the space for it."

Emily relaxed a little. "You could come and see it. Her. Him. Whatever it is. Maybe for a weekend."

"Maybe," she said noncommittally. "Not this weekend though, I'm—" She took a deep breath. "—I'm spending it with Avery."

"Who?"

"My friend, Mum. I told you about her."

"Oh. Right." She probably did. "I'm glad you're getting out, Jane. But I'd like it if you met someone. Aren't there any nice boys in Edinburgh?"

There was a long pause. Emily twisted the phone cord around her finger.

"I'm…I'm going out with Avery, Mum."

"Well, yes, I'm sure she's lovely, but you need more than just friends at your age. Is there no one in your classes you fancy?"

"Avery and I take Contemporary Lit. together. That's how we met."

Emily wondered if her daughter was being deliberately obtuse. Maybe she was just tired. "Well, don't leave it forever. You're young and gorgeous now, but if you whittle away these years you'll end up an old spinster like me."

"You're not a—" Jane heaved a heavy sigh. "Thanks, yeah, I'll think on that. I've got to go. Take care, Mum."

"Alright. Bye, Jane. I love you." But she was already gone.

Chapter IV

Mr Jonas stopped by the next morning with her firewood, like he did every second Friday throughout the autumn and winter months. Jonas was actually his first name, but Emily didn't find that out until she'd already been calling him Mr Jonas for three years. She gave him a bag of Jonagold apples, except she called them Jonas' Golds, and they laughed like they always did. She liked that Mr Jonas never made her feel old or silly, even though she always said Jonas' Golds like it was the first time.

"And how's Janey getting on in Edinburgh?" he said, as he piled up the wood on her porch and put the apples in his rucksack.

She's grand, yeah, Emily nearly said, because that's what you were supposed to say to the man without a proper last name who delivered your firewood and asked how your grown-up daughter was getting on in Edinburgh. But she surprised herself by saying, "I don't know, really. I ask her, and she asks me, but we never really seem to say anything."

He smiled, not like he was laughing at her, but just in a nice way, as if to say that he understood. "It's not easy by distance, is it? Maybe she'll come home for a visit soon and you can have a proper catching up."

"I'd like that," Emily said. "And how's Caroline doing?" Caroline was Mr Jonas' wife.

He hesitated. "She's...she's grand, yeah." Emily almost didn't catch the words because he had turned away from her. He straightened up and pulled the bag over his back.

"I hope she enjoys the apples," Emily said. "You know, I was speaking to another seller at the market, and she was telling me about these apple tarts her gran used to make with prosciutto and herbs and things..." but Mr Jonas was already turning to go. "Well, give her my best."

Mr Jonas nodded and smiled kind of halfway before taking off down the hill.

<u>Chapter V</u>
Emily took the linen bag out of the drawer. It wasn't that she was lonely, not exactly, but with Max and Janey both gone it

would be nice to have someone to talk to. Someone to show the September sunsets to like Max showed them to her. That familiar ache tugged on her insides, like an old war wound that rears its head long after the body has healed. It would be five years next spring.

She placed the dried rose aside, careful not to crush its delicate petals, and lined up the five vials—four full, one empty—and read the instructions again. It didn't look very difficult. She wasn't so convinced about the grave dirt, having been terrified by *The Monkey's Paw* back in school, but she didn't think it was meant to call on a real dead person. It was more like if you wanted someone brave you might choose a soldier, or for someone clever you might choose a novelist or a scientist or one of those people who made up the slogans for cereal boxes.

It wouldn't hurt just to have a look and see what was on offer. Jane wouldn't have to know.

Chapter VI

A brief, ferocious rain had cleared the cemetery of any picnickers and released a heady perfume of moss and blackberries and earth. Her guilt at not coming more often mingled with her wonder at how truly lovely it was, everything fresh and saturated with colour. Her boots made little squelches along the path.

Emily didn't recognise any of the names on the headstones. Though she supposed the ones with the crypts and the statues of angels and things were probably quite rich; that might do. She passed a stone that said, 'Poet, Scholar, and Beloved Friend'. Would she fancy a poet to scribble her sweet nothings as if she were a girl of seventeen?

Her feet knew the way even as her mind wandered. It was Jane who'd found the apple tree and insisted he be buried under it. Emily pushed the bruised, fallen fruit aside and knelt in the grass. The recent rain soaked through her trousers in an instant.

"Hello, darling."

She ran her finger across the etched letters. Moss was beginning to blossom. Max would have liked that. She took the vial out of her coat pocket, suddenly feeling silly.

"It's just…it's hard being so alone all the time," she told him. She turned the vial over in her hands, watching the label wink in and out of view. *You were always the strong one*, she wanted to say, but the words seemed so petulant, so small. A gust of wind blew through the treetops and a cascade of raindrops fell from the apple tree. They made a thunderous racket for a moment, then were silent.

She put the empty vial back in her pocket. Then she stood, brushing bits of grass off her legs, and left the cemetery.

Chapter VII
Emily set up her stall at the market the next day and looked for the nice woman with the perfumes. She wasn't there.

Chapter VIII
The week was warm; Emily still had lots of firewood left when Mr Jonas came again. She greeted him from the porch.

"That's lovely. We'll have a right cosy time while Jane's here."

He brightened. "Is she coming for a visit, then?"

"She is, yeah. Next week. She's bringing a friend with her too."

Mr Jonas raised an eyebrow. "A gentleman friend?"

Emily sighed. "No, nothing like that. A girlfriend of hers, Avery something-or-other. Seems quite keen on her. I'm glad she's made a nice friend." As she said it, she wondered if it was the truth. She'd been looking forward to her time with Jane, just the two of them. But then, it was good that Jane had someone to spend time with. The right man would come along in time. There was no rush.

Mr Jonas was giving her a funny look. "I'm sure the three of you will have lots to talk about." He stacked the firewood up on the pile, which was only a little smaller than last time.

"Did Caroline enjoy the apples?" she asked.

Mr Jonas straightened. He didn't meet her eyes. Instead he ran a hand through his hair. It was quite nice hair, she noticed, for a man his age.

"Mr Jonas, is something wrong?"

He sighed, crossed his arms, and uncrossed them again. "Caroline left."

Emily's mind went curiously blank. "What do you mean, she left?"

"She went back home. During the summer."

"Is she—" *coming back?* But she saw the look on his face. "I'm so sorry. I didn't know."

Mr Jonas shrugged. "It had been coming for a while. Things weren't so easy for her here." He pulled his rucksack on. "Have a nice time with Jane and her friend." He turned towards the hill.

"Mr Jonas," Emily said suddenly. "That is...Jonas." His name tasted oddly naked without the 'Mr' in front of it.

He turned back to look at her.

"Would you like to stay for a cup of tea? There are some lovely sunsets here."

He blinked, and a slow smile began in his eyes and made its way down to his lips.

He took off his rucksack and laid it by the door as they went inside.

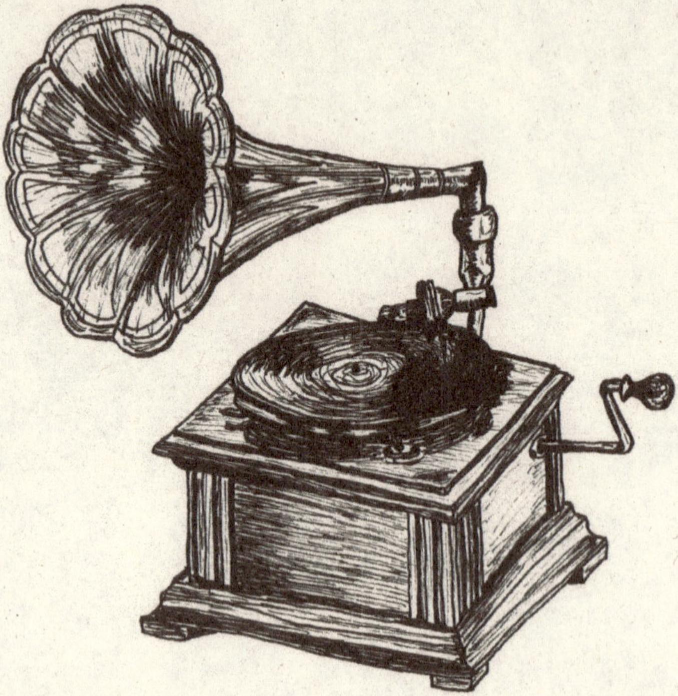

The Edge of Morning

When I died, I lost:
1 pair of red patent Repetto ballet flats, size 36 (€280)
1500 or so books, including a first edition copy of *Peter Pan* (est. total €16,000)
1 unfinished poetry collection, provisionally titled *Night-blooming Roses* (€50 or so)
1 city-centre apartment, with balcony (priceless)
1 future
1 vintage gramophone (value unknown)

***

When we moved in together, he brought most of his furniture with him. I had two suitcases—one of clothes, the other of books—and a vintage gramophone secured to the top of the small suitcase with bootlaces.

I put the clothes in one corner, and the books in another corner, and the gramophone beneath the window, and thought, *Yes. Home.*

I am home.

I'm a first-year undergrad sitting in one of those after-theatre bars where I don't know anybody. It's too loud and it smells like spilled liquor. I'm sipping orange juice because it's the only thing they serve with no alcohol in it. My housemate, who begged me to come so she wouldn't be alone, is late.

Everybody seems to know everybody else. There is a disproportionate number of fedoras.

You could read something too, she says. It's chill, everyone's really supportive.

The very thought makes me dizzy. I never share my poems with anyone.

Well, just come and cheer me on then, she says. And I say, Yeah, okay, because I have nothing else to do on a Saturday night.

The bartender thinks I'm pregnant. She glanced at my stomach when I asked for orange juice.

Driving? she says.

I shake my head, realising a beat too late I should have just said yes.

Someone's stepping onto the little dais that serves as a stage. He speaks into the mic and welcomes everyone. My housemate isn't here and if I try to leave now, everyone will stare at me.

He's wearing a fedora over a shock of golden hair. I've never seen that colour on a man before. His pinstripe jacket is all sharp lines to make up for the softness of his face. He is not beautiful, but something about him makes me wonder if I could be. Like I, the bartender, everyone in the room has been stunningly beautiful this whole time only no one thought to tell us. I wonder what it would be like to feel the softness of him beneath my fingers.

He recites a poem into the mic. It has words like *ephemeral*, *superfluous*, and *artifice*. I count *artifice* twice. I don't understand it very well, but I like the sound the words make all tangled up together. I want to wrap them around myself and fall asleep in them.

~·~

It's two in the morning and we're walking near College Green over a fresh dusting of snow. I keep looking over my shoulder at the marks our boots have left behind—two perfect rows of silhouettes on a canvas tinted lamplight-bronze. I feel that we have in some small way marked the world as our own; that this still, silent night is offering it to us in all its limitless potential.

~·~

"Your mum called," he says one evening, when I arrive home from work. "There's a message."

Our home has grown full of more books than I could ever fit in a suitcase. Cheap paperbacks and first editions scoured from bookshop basements stand proudly side by side. Everywhere I turn are small reminders that I am here, I am real: wildflowers that I picked for him, hanging upside down to dry; a bronze plaque with a claddagh on it that I found at a charity shop for six euro; a poem I wrote, scribbled onto a restaurant napkin and framed. My poetry is not refined and elevated like his, but it makes me feel as though I have given some small gift to the world, some payment for taking up space in it.

My feet ache from a ten-hour shift at the boutique, but I pause in the doorway. My mother never calls.

It's not until much later, after dinner, after asking about his day, after making love slowly and quietly on the balcony under the stars, that I listen to the message. My mother has heard from an old mutual friend that my father is ill. Very ill.

Maybe you should call him, she says.

I thought the world would hurt less when I was dead.

I thought the agony of loss would soften into dull-edged oblivion. I thought that all the questions I had would become, if not answered, less important than they'd been before.

Death was less like oblivion and more like anhedonia. This was a word I learned from one of his poems. I wandered through the apartment, my ghostly feet passing through cardboard boxes as he packed up our life. I watched him lock the claddagh away with packing tape, untie the wildflowers and press them into the compost bin. Little by little, the walls were stripped down until it was like I was never there at all.

He sold the gramophone. A man with thick plastic glasses and sideburns came to take it away. I tried to stop him, but my voice was an empty murmur on the wind.

The autumn I turn fourteen, the guidance counsellor calls me into her office.

She says, this needs to stop.

I blink up at her, shuffling through possibilities in my mind. I have no idea what she's talking about.

She says, you can't be drinking alcohol before school. You're here to learn, and if you can't bring yourself to do that, we need to think about whether or not you should be here at all.

I'm still completely at sea. I don't drink alcohol, I say. I add that I'm fourteen, and wonder if she's confused me for someone else.

The counsellor gives me an impatient look and says, your teachers can smell it on your clothes.

Understanding crashes into me. For a brief moment I consider trying to explain my mother, the scent of her that clings to the walls, the white-hot anger that flares and roars without warning. The way I get through one day at a time by making myself small.

The moment passes, and instead I just look down and nod.

That night I get into the shower and scrub and scrub and scrub. I start keeping extra clothes in the back of my locker.

⁂

Two months after we move in together, *Bindweed Quarterly* writes to me to say they want to publish one of my poems.

I read the message three times. Somebody wants to put my words in a real literary journal. Once my hands are steady and I'm sure I didn't imagine it, I run into the other room to tell him.

He puts his arms around me. "I'm so proud of you," he says. I try to think if anyone has been proud of me before, and come up blank.

To celebrate, we put a record on the gramophone. The cool cascade of "Minor Swing" floats into the air. He offers me his hand, and together we kick our heels up in the living room, laughing and tripping over each other's feet. I'm so happy I feel as though my heart could burst.

My leaving ceremony is about to begin, and I'm the last one to enter the auditorium. I stand outside in the car park, in a shimmering dress I've borrowed from the school's drama department, scanning the row of vehicles again and again. When at last I hear the voices settle I think, *maybe he's already inside*.

My mother is there, sober and smiling. Her handbag occupies the seat beside her. She catches my eye and her smile dims. Later, she will call my father and yell into the phone, and I'll want to tell her *it's fine, it's no big deal*, but the words won't come.

He does make it seven months later. I brush my hair and plait it, then loosen it, then plait it again. As we walk by the seaside, he tells me that his girlfriend is pregnant.

I didn't know my father had a girlfriend.

We spend the afternoon wandering through the shopping centre, looking at baby clothes.

"I thought you hated the guy," he says, when I tell him about the message.

I don't hate him, I reply. I turn the words over in my mouth, prod them with my tongue, searching for the off-flavours of a lie. Hate is too simplistic, I decide. A single, reverberating note.

"Are you going to go see him?"

I haven't seen my father in more than ten years. His daughter is thirteen now. I saw her in a songwriting competition on TV.

I say I don't know, and put the kettle on. I'll think about it later. I've got time.

❦

I learn how to tell the bad days from the Really Bad Days. My mother hurts me very rarely; more often it's dishes, wine glasses, picture frames. I wait until she disappears into her bedroom, and then I pick my way around the broken shards, knowing they'll have been cleaned up by the time I get back.

Today she doesn't disappear into her bedroom. Instead, she knocks on my door.

Just a minute, I say, I'm getting changed.

I know I don't have very long, so I grab every breakable thing I see and shove it under my bed.

Come in, I say, as if everything's fine. The room suddenly feels very small.

She asks me a question. At this point I know that anything I say will be the wrong thing to say, so I don't answer. The silence hums, crackles, snaps.

It's like watching a tornado trapped inside the body of a five-foot-tall woman. I stay very, very still as it tears across my bookshelves, my dresser, pulls the magazine cutouts from the walls. A thumbtack rains down with them, and I make a mental note not to step on it later. She yanks a mirror off the wall and I think, *Drat. I should have grabbed that.*

She's breathing hard, and for a moment I think it might be over. Then her eyes land on the gramophone. I stiffen, and my fingers tighten at my side. I force myself not to move. To react will make it all so much worse.

The gramophone topples over with a crack. The wide brass horn clatters as it snaps off the wooden base. She kicks it across the room. I can hardly breathe.

The horn is still ringing distantly, and as it fades, the gale dies down. My mother looks around at the carnage as if seeing it for the first time. She chokes back a sob and runs from the room. I hear the front door open and shut, the rattling of keys.

I don't know why she's upset, I think. *It wasn't* her *gramophone.*

When the house is still, I take the brass horn in my arms and finally allow myself to cry.

When my poetry pamphlet wins a chapbook contest—€200 and publication—I start to notice that something's wrong.

"That's great." His voice is flat and he doesn't look at me.

I'd been thinking about the red ballet flats I wanted to buy with my winnings, but I stop and frown.

Isn't it? I say.

He's not having much luck with his submissions. Modern poetry is too subjective; it doesn't appreciate form. His use of figurative language and Keatsean rhetoric passes over the heads of most editors.

Privately, I wonder if his aim is too narrow. He submits only to *the New Yorker, Threepenny, the Paris Review*. I once suggested trying some smaller magazines, but he told me that would be a waste because it would use up first publication rights without any exposure or prestige in return. He said this like it should be obvious. I said, oh, ok.

It's just a chapbook, I tell him. It's like a glorified business card.

I'm not sure why I'm saying these things. I thought he would be happy.

He smiles, and nods, and everything is alright again. Can we put on some music? I say.

"I'm exhausted," he says. "I'm going to bed."

I drifted through memories.

Some of them seemed more real to me here, in this in-between place, than they did while I was living them. The sharp crack of breaking glass; the creeping chill of loneliness in a high school car park; the simmering terror of loss.

I looked at the girl I was and understood, for the first time, how those moments shaped the woman she grew to become. I understood that when my mother did those things to our home, she was stopping herself from doing them to me. I understood that my father saw in his new daughter a chance to start again, free from mistakes and the weight of lost years.

I understood that the man I loved was never going to love me in the way that I loved him.

I curled up in a ball of smoke and shadow and ached for all the things I didn't understand.

The phone rings in my ear. It has a tinny, faraway sound and I imagine it reaching through the void of space, across highways and rivers, to the farmhouse my father shares with his wife and daughter. His family.

I don't know what to say. Sorry to hear that you're dying? Do you need anything? Why did you leave me?

I have thirty years of unspoken questions, and all of them turn to ash in my mouth.

His daughter answers. I recognise her voice from the TV show.

Hello, she says.

Hi. Hello, I struggle for words. Is Dad there?

Who's this, she says.

I tell her my name.

There is a long pause. Then she says, who?

I hang up.

Not long after I turn nineteen, my mother announces she's moving in with her boyfriend. I see her less and less. Sometimes she's gone for days at a time.

I can't keep living like this, she says.

You don't appreciate anything I do for you, she says.

You don't talk to me. You don't look at me.

It's like living with a stranger.

I fix my eyes on the frayed threading on my jeans. It's not a Really Bad Day, so if I'm careful, I can dodge the worst of it.

She says some other things too, but I don't hear because I'm busy mentally sifting through my bank account, wondering how I'm going to pay for this apartment on my own.

She leaves most of the furniture behind, and I sell it piece by piece to get by. Dining table: €75. Three chairs: €40.

Standing lamp: €8. I eat ready meals standing up at the kitchen countertop. Soon the only thing left is a clumsily repaired gramophone, looking like a relic from another age.

For a while, he keeps his other women hidden from me. After a few months he stops bothering, and I can smell them on his clothes, feel the shape of them in his touch. I stop telling him when my poetry is accepted, and then I stop sending it out altogether, but I'm too late. The damage is done. I've already driven a wedge between us that I can never take back.

I want so much to be what he needs, but I don't know how.

We lie beside each other in the dark, and I trace the shape of him in the shadows.

Please don't leave me, I whisper. It's so quiet that I'm not sure if I really said it at all, or if I only imagined it.

When I'm seven, I go to stay with my father for a week in the country. He comes to pick me up in a mud-splattered truck cancerous with rust, and I delight in the novelty of sitting in a vehicle. The city whips by the window until it becomes golden farmland.

There is so much space, not only outside but in his three-bedroomed, high-ceilinged house, that I am dizzy with it. I want to explore every corner of this new world, but my eyes are drawn to a vintage gramophone standing in the corner.

That was your grandad's, he says. Here, let's put something on.

My father chooses a record. Do you know Django Reinhardt?

I shake my head.

He lowers the needle and music fills the room. It's like nothing I've ever heard before. He bows and offers me his hand and I giggle, suddenly shy.

I like feeling his big, safe hands over my small ones as we dance around the room. Happiness bubbles up inside me like fizzy pop. I want to stay in this farmhouse and dance with him forever.

When the song ends, I make him play it over and over again.

Afterwards he says, you can take that with you, if you want. Set it up in your room. I never use it.

My happiness turns to awe. I've never owned anything so wonderful in all of my long seven years. I imagine how it will look in my bedroom, catching the first rays of morning light.

Thank you, I say nervously. The words feel too small for such a momentous gift.

Can I try putting a record on? I say.

He teaches me how to lift the needle, suspended in mid-air, and then let go. Never put it down on the record he says, or you might scratch it. Just hold it in your fingers and let go.

It takes me a few tries to get it right. "Minor Swing" fills the room. I grab his hand and we dance until it's time for dinner.

⁓

He's going to stay with his parents for the weekend. He says he hasn't seen them in a while. They live three hours away in a commuter town with gardens and red-brick houses. I ask if he wants me to go with him.

He's silent so long I become tongue-tied. I know that whatever I say next, no matter what it is, will be the wrong thing.

Finally he says, "I've already asked someone." He pushes his dinner around with his fork. "I'd like them to meet her."

There's nothing I can say that won't be the wrong thing to say, that won't tear us farther apart. Suddenly I'm choking and I can't stop. There is a rushing deep inside of me, and I think of the tornado that tore through my mother all those years ago. For the first time I realise that it lives in me too.

I don't remember putting my shoes on, but I am outside in the grey afternoon light. The world has a hazy, underwater quality to it. I stumble into the street and hear a car horn, loud and insistent and sharp.

In books they always say, *It all happened so fast*. It doesn't happen fast. There's a moment, a shimmering prism of time, in which I could step out of harm's way. I hold the moment in my hands and stare into it, and the moment stares back.

Nah, screw it, I think finally. *It's better this w*

༺❦༻

The man in the hipster glasses loaded my gramophone into the back of a truck. The truck said, *Robinson's Antiques*. I watched from the upstairs window.

The truck idled, like a purring monster, waiting.

I walked through the gutted apartment, touching misty fingers to empty bookshelves, barren walls. The only safe, happy home I'd ever known. I wondered where he would go now. Who he would become.

When the truck roared to life, I was there like a breath of wind. I did not look back.

<hr />

Robinson's Antiques is dusty and cluttered and filled with stories. I wander through the soft, welcoming silence on a faded carpet the colour of snow. My steps make no sound.

I like the quiet.

After the shop closes and the salespeople go home—to families, loved ones, lives—I hold the gramophone needle carefully in mid-air and let go. "Minor Swing" spills into the dark.

I spin myself into the lonely golden glow of the streetlamp, and kick my heels up, and think, *Yes. Home.*

I am home.

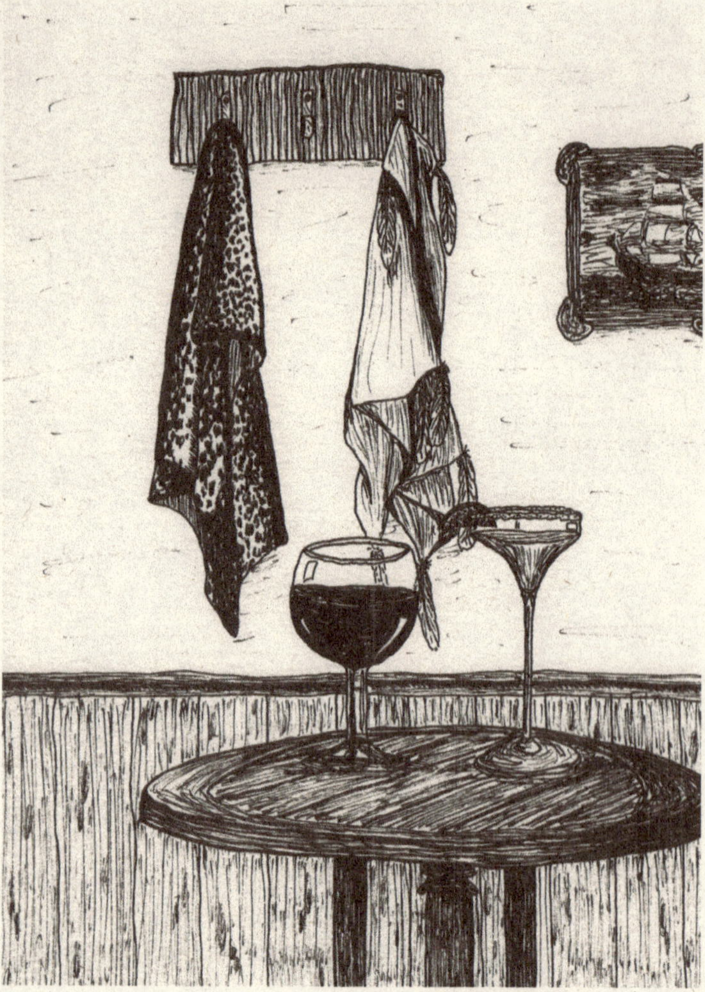

The Selkie and the Swan Maiden

They're a peculiar pair, the two that come into the pub together every Thursday night. She is dark-haired and slender, just shy of gauntness, with wine-stained lips and fingers like a piano player. *She* is short and squat like somebody's mother, with the pale, pale hair one normally sees only on very small children.

She always orders the blackberry wine, made locally by a family-owned vineyard from organic berries handpicked in August and September. *She* orders a sidecar. Never more than one drink each, and somehow they make them stretch from seven to midnight. They talk about their husbands (both tiresome), their days (both dreary), and sometimes, when the night grows deep and the streets grow still, of home.

They watch the girls from the nearby university order pretty pink drinks that they position flatteringly in the overhead lights. With wistful half-smiles the women say to each other, "Were we ever truly that young?"

"I remember," she says (it always starts like this), "I remember playing catch-me with the gulls that followed the fishing boats around the bay. They were always so clumsy, so slow."

"I remember," *she* says, "flying up to the sun with my brothers and seeing who could break off the biggest piece to take home. We were never sure who won, though, because they'd always burn out before we could reach the ground."

She's heard this story before, of course, but she tilts her head and nods as though it's the first time, because that's what friends do.

"I remember," she says, sipping blackberry wine, "leaving my skin on the sand that very first time. The world was so cold. I didn't expect it to be so cold."

"Yes." *She* nods in agreement. The cold is something they both remember. "I believed that discarding my feathers would bring me closer to the sun. I didn't understand that to be in a woman's shape was to be vulnerable. I was so young."

"And then he was there. My sweet Eamon, looking for words of poetry in the tide. I thought perhaps the world was not so cold after all."

"I'd have given my Peter my coat of feathers willingly, if he'd asked. I'd have followed him to the lost kingdom below just to be near him."

The women sigh, watching the university girls lean in together with smiles yet undimmed by the fleeting attentions of men.

Eamon is no longer the idealistic young artist that wandered the coastline alone, all those years ago. Now he wears tailored suits and works in an office twenty storeys above the street, with broad bright windows and a trunk bound with thick iron hinges. She tried to open it once. Just once. It was sealed by two numerical locks. The key to her skin was in her husband's head.

She was not so fortunate. Her Peter's eyes grew farther and farther away with time, smudged behind whiskey and pewter-grey cigarette smoke. It was such a little thing, a red ember glowing against the darkness and left to smoulder on a dry oak countertop. *It could have been a lot worse*, they said, especially the big man with the yellow hat and the flashing red truck. *You were lucky.* The neighbourhood gathered on the street, watching the flames lick the sky above the house with her feathers inside of it. None of them pulled their eyes away from the glow long enough to see six swans circling in the smoke overhead, shedding tears for the sister who would never fly again.

The night grows long and low, as it always does, and the women set their glasses down. They have lives to return to (she to a high rise townhouse, *she* to a rundown council flat), and men who love them still, in their own way, even if their memories of who their wives once were and how they met have become unaccountably dim. They leave the bar walking close, but not touching, and greet the cool night air together. If one feels the lilt of the breeze and remembers the feel of wind under her wings, or if one catches a hint of sea salt in the air and thinks of languid summer days basking on the skerry, they say nothing. They simply turn away and melt into the hard, cold world that has become their home.

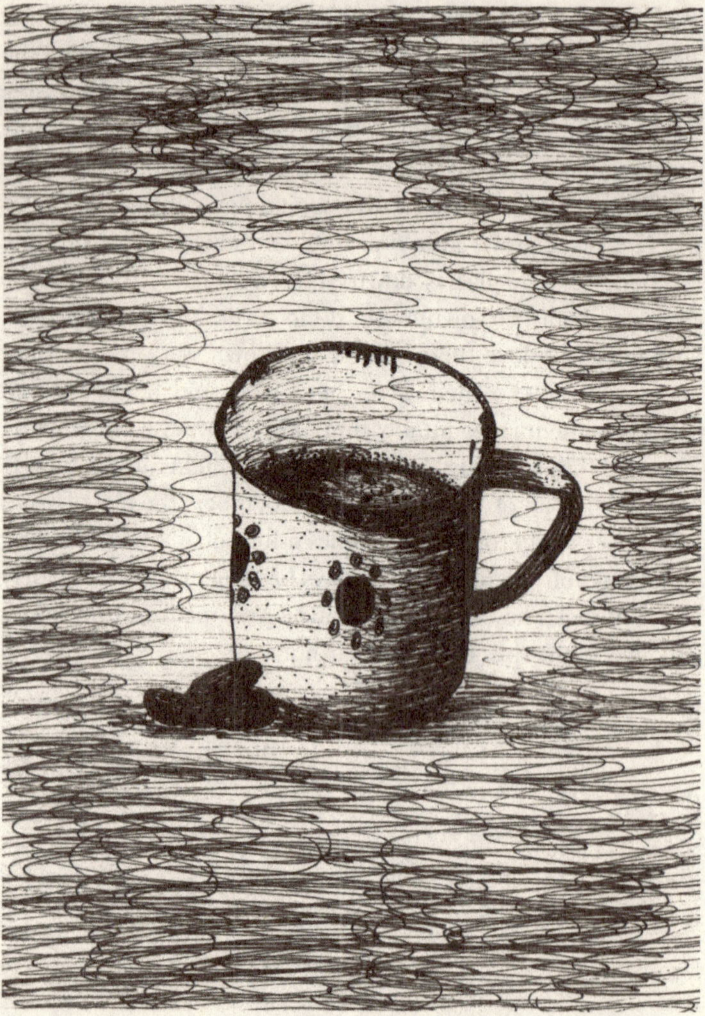

After the Fall

Dried cacao beans simmer on the stovetop until they split, the shells sloughing off like dead skin. Their heady, earthy scent mixes with the incense I prepared of cinnamon and motherwort and cacao husks and chilli. Together they whisper stories of long-forgotten battlefields, of blood promises and old gods.

I break the beans into pieces, stone on stone, picking out the frail, paper-like shells. The preparation is as much a part of the ritual as any spoken word—roasting the rare criollo beans by hand, grinding the nibs to a paste, each turn of pestle on mortar like the turning of a cog. Or a key.

The cacao, of course, is not the first food used to unlock doors between worlds. Six pomegranate seeds once tore open a gate to Hades; nine sheaves of wheat formed a bridge to Avalon. In another time, in another place, a wardrobe made of apple wood linked one world to another. But today there are no apple trees or garnet-coloured seeds. Only the slow, purposeful grinding of cacao by candlelight.

It is the slowness that makes me ache with longing and rage. But these things cannot be rushed.

The beans have passed through many hands between the rainforested Cacahoatán region of Mexico and my cramped kitchen in South London. It's dizzying to think of the road they have taken, the road *I* have taken, to arrive at this moment. As the nibs break down into a paste, I hold his image in my mind as I last saw him. Clear blue eyes and a handsome face unlined by the hardships of the world. A smile playing around the edges of his lips as if somehow, despite everything we had been through, the world was still one big, beautiful riddle to be solved.

Once the chocolate is slick and smooth, I mix it with milk and thistle honey and warm the blend gently on the stove. The stirring soothes my unsteady hands. As I pour it into a chipped mug I whisper a dedication to Quetzalcoatl, bringer of all things, a prayer for his blood to keep me safe.

Years ago, before my sister was born, we had a neighbour who would come by while my parents were at work—Claudette, who must have been at least ninety and spoke with a French accent softened by time. How she ended up in the dirty streets of Tulse Hill I never knew and never thought to ask. She taught me about the plants that grew in the back garden, and skimmed the edges of the pavements, and glimmered in the supermarket. Lavender, she explained, would calm an argument. Dandelions, *les dents de lion*, would make me brave. Apples, figs, even potatoes had their own earthly magic.

"What about chocolate?" I asked, only half-joking. My favourite was Cadbury Creme Eggs.

But the woman gave me a serious look. "Chocolate is old magic," she said. "It is darkness and passion and blood. Hope that you will never need it."

At seven years old, I had not understood. I understand now.

The room grows dim with incense smoke. I sit and pick up the blade I'd set aside. I've never been good at pain, at taking risks. It was my sister, Millie, who was always the fearless one, jumping off the swings too early, coming home with new bruises and scrapes and ready to do it all over again. I grit my teeth and pull the knife across my palm.

The wound gapes raw and ragged against the heel of my hand. I take a deep breath and wait for the pain to ebb. Cacao magic is warrior magic, and the place I am going will have no patience for weakness.

I whisper one last, desperate prayer to Xōchiquetzal, to Coatlicue, maiden and mother, and lift the cup to my lips.

In some far-distant place, I feel the smooth ceramic between my hands and the cool wooden floorboards beneath my legs. The sensations are muted, distant, like viewing them through a dirty window. Here I am on my feet, and barren red earth stretches out in every direction. The taste of chocolate lingers on my lips.

I hold my hand close to my chest and a perilous flutter of fear climbs up my throat. I don't know how long the drink will protect me, how long it will be until the dead notice a living thing, a bleeding thing, in their midst. All I need is to find him, speak to him. Just one moment.

For that I will brave anything this shadow land can throw at me.

I whisper his name into the dead air: William Mahoney. It seems like such a respectable name, the kind that might have an old Irish granny waiting for it somewhere in Connemara, wondering why he never came home.

I thought I was alone in this strange landscape, but here and there I see flickers of other Afterlands. They tangle up together like double-exposed photographs. On one side, the River Styx glimmers in and out of sight; on the other, the verdant fields of Tír na nÓg sprawl across the icy expanse of Hel. And then I begin to hear them, the cries of the damned, their humanity stripped away by their own twisted memories. I think of William somewhere like that, unable to speak, unable to remember, and my heart twists until I cannot breathe.

There are other things lurking in the fringes, too. Shadowy, ethereal things. Hungry things.

I focus my eyes ahead and remind myself of why I've come. The ache to feel him beneath my touch, just once. To dig my nails into his flesh and watch him bleed.

The shadows hover nearby and examine my hand with curiosity. In that distant place, I raise the coffee mug to my lips and taste the smoky-earthy sweetness of Quetzalcoatl's blood. The transition is disorienting, like too much wine too quickly, and I fight to keep my feet rooted in the Afterland. As long as the cacao flows through me, the shadows will not harm me. Probably.

The last and only time I saw William Mahoney, we stared at each other from across a crowded courtroom floor. My mother and father stood beside me. Her face was bloated from tears that never stopped falling, my father's gaunt and grey. I thought I could handle it, being there across the room from him, giving the nightmare a human face, but I was wrong. My father dragged me screaming from the courtroom, screaming until the words no longer made sense to my own ears, screaming because I didn't know what else to do and didn't know how to stop.

In the end, William Mahoney was convicted of murdering three girls, none older than twelve. Two of the bodies had been recovered. Millie's was not one of them.

My family agreed to a deal: Mahoney would tell us where to find my sister in exchange for a reduced sentence—fifteen years instead of a lifetime. Maybe less. My father hated the idea, hated the thought of setting a monster loose on the streets, but my mother's tears finally wore him down.

I just want to say goodbye.

I didn't say anything, but privately I agreed. It was a fair price. But then William had been found dead in his prison cell with a switchblade in his throat.

I whisper his name again into the air. Rust-red dust rises and glitters in the thin sepia light. The landscape is so empty, so vast, and a flicker of uncertainty worms its way in just before I crest a sunset-coloured hilltop and see him.

William Mahoney sits alone in the dust, his eyes vacant. Even here, in this wasteland of broken souls, he is beautiful. What did he promise those girls, I wonder. What stories did he tell them in the dark? Maybe they made their own promises just by looking at him, the way girls so often do when they know nothing of the world.

I know my sister is dead. To let myself believe otherwise would kill me. But maybe, if I can learn where she's hidden, my family and I can finally find peace.

We can say goodbye.

The shadows shift at the periphery of my vision, straining towards my bleeding hand. There is no time here, which means there is no coagulation, no healing. In my far-away body, I fortify myself with another sip of chocolate. I blink, reorient myself, and go over to William. I sit down cross-legged in the dust.

He looks up. William doesn't look tortured at all. He looks healthy, his eyes still that vivid, disarming blue. I feel a flush of white-hot rage, as if he shouldn't deserve colour after he'd taken all of it away from my family. But not yet. There will be time for rage after.

"William Mahoney," I say, with a soft smile. "You're a difficult man to find."

His eyes skim me up and down, a series of quick judgments flickering one after the other. "Ah, well, our past catches up with us all in the end, doesn't it?" But he says it with a grin, mocking himself, mocking the world, mocking the great mysteries that brought us both here face to face.

He tilts his head to one side. "So, what did they get you with?" He must have seen the confusion on my face, because he continues, "What did you do to get stuck in this hole?"

"Made a deal with a god." I wonder what he sees when he looks around him. What hell does he believe in? What stories kept young William Mahoney up at night?

He barks a short, mirthless laugh. "You wouldn't be the first to make that mistake, my dear. Don't worry. You're pretty and sweet. They love that kind of thing."

And he had loved it too. Pretty and sweet. Just on the cusp of womanhood, childhood innocence beginning to crack and reveal the fears underneath.

"How many?" I ask, startling myself. It doesn't matter how many. That isn't why I'm here.

"How many what?"

I hesitate. "How many girls?" It comes out in a whisper, broken. He was convicted of three, but everyone knew there were more. More missing girls, more buried stories. It was only after my sister that he got sloppy.

He meets my eyes for a moment, then shrugs and looks away. "I didn't count."

I dig my nails into my bloody palm until the pain clears my head.

"Anyway," he says, "I won't be hanging around much longer. My lawyer has a deal on the table."

I open my mouth, then close it. It takes a moment for it to click.

The arsehole doesn't even know he's dead.

I focus on my hands, those other hands in that other place, and lift the chocolate to my lips. The cup is empty. I'm wasting time.

"Tell me about this deal," I say. I try to keep my voice light, two conspirators locked away, two lost souls together in the dark.

He leans back against his elbows, as if he were on a riverbank instead of in a jail cell—or the sands of hell. "The usual. Information."

"About the girls?" I wish I had more time. If he senses desperation, he will play with me and spit me out. I will lose him.

The shadows gather at the edges of my vision, drawn by the scent of my blood. From somewhere in the distance comes the fluttering of wings.

He glances down, noticing my hand for the first time. "Someone get rough with you?"

"Something like that." I run my thumb across my palm, where the blood is beginning to pool. It comes away red. "What information?"

He closes his eyes, and a slow smile plays over his face. "You ever kill anyone before?"

I tamp down my frustration. "Not yet," I say. Then I amend myself. "No." *No, I am not like you.*

He doesn't look at me, but his smile broadens into a grin. "Don't worry," he says. "You will."

I wasn't worried, I want to snap, but his calm unnerves me. "What makes you think that?"

He opens his eyes again and examines my face, as though memorising its contours and angles. "I can see it. Your anger. That's where it begins. Before it becomes play, before it's a game, a hunt, whatever you think it is, long before that, it's anger. It's fire burning so hot it whites out everything else, and I see it under your skin. It's only a matter of time."

I stare at him. There is so much I want to say. *I will never be like you.* I imagine raking my nails down his face, feeling his hot blood sink into my cuticles, the longing so intense it makes my breath catch.

Instead, I say, "You're wrong."

"I'll make you a deal," he says lazily, and closes his eyes again. "Tell me your secret, and I'll tell you mine. I want to know what debaucherous atrocity you committed to get tossed in here with me. Not that I'm complaining, mind. The scenery was getting dull."

His closed eyes give me a chance to study his face in return. It's the kind that will stay young forever, with full lips I may have fallen for in another life. Hatred makes my vision swim.

"Someone hurt my family," I say. "The police punished him, but it wasn't enough."

He opens his eyes and gives me an appraising look. "It never is."

"Your turn," I say, smoothing down my voice like I'd smooth a wrinkled dress. "What information could be so valuable that it would buy you a ticket out?" I'm careful not to look at him.

"There was one they were still looking for. They had enough to book me for it but not enough to find her. I agreed to draw them a treasure map in exchange for an early pass."

After the Fall

I take a deep breath, the taste of chocolate on my tongue. Every step of my preparations have led me to this moment. My mother's tears, the haunted hollowness in my father's eyes. The sound of my screams still ringing in my ears, still ringing for weeks after. I walked through the very gates of hell for one simple question.

"Where is she?"

William grinned. "Sorry. Trade secret."

Lost.

Millie was lost.

For a moment, the walls around my resolve tilt. It can't be over. I won't let it be over. I will claw him apart with my bare hands.

But the shadows at the edges of the world are stirring.

"Well, you sure ran the police in circles. It must have been somewhere pretty clever." I had hoped to appeal to his vanity, but my voice sounds thin and desperate to my own ears. My plan is coming apart. It's happening too fast.

He gives me a hard look, and a shadow of recognition passes behind his eyes. "Who did you say you were again?"

I study him a moment longer. His eyes are clear and blue and shrewd, his nose gently aquiline, like a hunter's. I imagine him taking Millie by the hand, making her laugh. It would have been easy. I imagine all the others who were never found, all the broken families, all the broken lives. Then I let my eyes flutter closed. I breathe. In the world beyond, I tilt the cup way back and suck out the last few drops of bitter chocolate, coating my lips with it, inhaling the smoky-sweet scent one last time. *Quetzalcoatl, give me strength.*

I open my eyes.

"Do you know where you are, William Mahoney?"

He gives me that boyish grin again, though the caution doesn't leave his eyes. "City's finest. The Ritz was booked out for the weekend."

"No."

He frowns and looks away.

"You screwed up," I say. "Made someone angry. A lot of people angry, actually." I keep my voice steady and slow, even as my heart jumps. "But one was all it took."

He looks back at me, and I see it, then—the fear, deep and primordial, hidden behind layers and layers of self-delusion.

Perhaps a part of him does know, after all.

"Do you see them?" I look towards the edges of the dust land. The shadows are beginning to take shape with angles and edges, sharp talons and sheets of darkness that beat against the still air.

He tears his eyes away from me, squinting as though looking at the sun. The wan reddish light of the Afterland is fading.

"They're coming for you."

The fear shines brighter in his eyes now, like a shark rising to the surface of the sea.

"No, I have a deal, my lawyer said—"

"I'll make you a new one," I say. "Tell me where my sister is, and I'll get you out of here."

I watch the wheels turn in his head. His eyes flicker over me, no doubt looking for Millie in my face. Maybe remembering what she had been like in her last moments. The feeling of her delicate bones beneath his soft, boyish hands.

"You can do that?"

"Think faster, William."

He looks around frantically at the darkening sky. I stand, brushing dust off my trousers, and turn away. Though it kills me, I take a step. Then another.

"Wait!"

I stop, relief flooding my chest.

William stands too. "There's an outdoor cellar behind the swimming pool. They used to keep life jackets and stuff there, but it's abandoned now. That's where you'll find them."

I turn, my heart pounding. William has gone ash-pale. Red dust clings to his clothes.

"Thank you," I say gently. I dig my nails into the heel of my hand and force the wound apart. Fresh blood wells up, sticky and hot. I reach out and press it to his open throat, feel it smear beneath my touch.

He stares at me, wide eyed.

For a wild, surreal moment, I'm tempted to kiss him, to make him feel as caged and helpless as she was, to taste the mingled blood and chocolate before his soul is ripped apart.

I don't. I am not like him.

"Goodbye, William," I whisper.

I pull back my hand. It leaves a vivid red stain behind, like a gaping mouth. The air comes alive with beating wings.

"Wait! *We had a deal!*"

I step back and watch the shadows descend. His screams echo in my ears as I open my eyes.

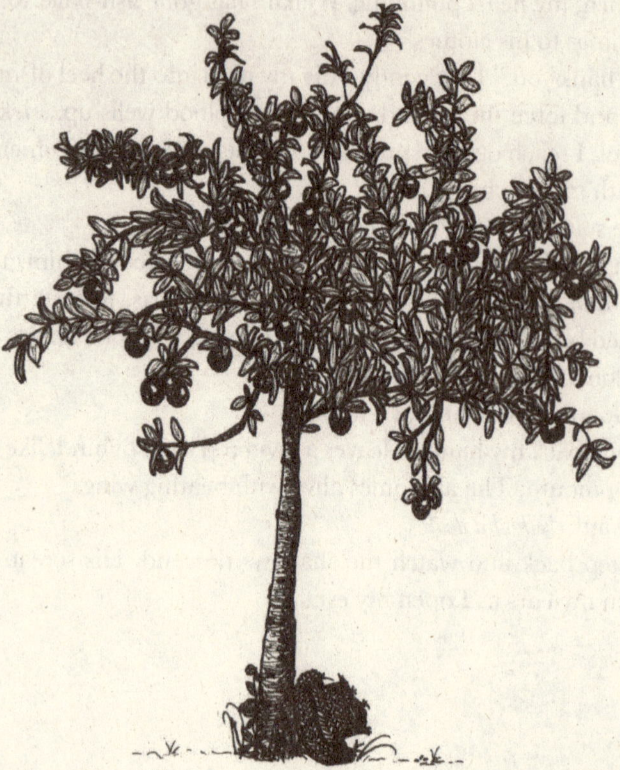

Apple Seeds

That first fruit was always special.
A celebration, a tradition left behind
from childhood—hers, not mine;
I was city-bred. She'd lived in a farmhouse
in a town that had no name
because, she said,
it didn't exist anymore.

Three equal pieces:
one for you, she'd say,
one for me, and one
for the apple tree man.

Cut from the first harvest and the last
before the frost came,
given in tithe,
given in tribute.
A superstition carried
from the old country
(she was never quite certain
which old country).

Frail Little Embers

I wasn't from an old country.
I didn't always understand
how she could walk barefoot
through stinging nettles,
with chains of buttercups
wrapped around her feet;
or why the bees would gather
just to listen to her voice.

I didn't need to understand
because she made the world beautiful,
and that was how they did things
in the old country.

❧

We bought the house
in late September.
The garden was strewn
with bindweed and ivy

and two trees: a maple, gnarled
and hunched like an old woman
with moss and lichen
all down its back.

An apple tree:
small,
unassuming.

Apple Seeds

On autumn days we'd sit outside
and guess which apples it would bring.
She liked the way the words took shape
inside the contours of her mouth:

Bramley,
Braeburn,
Pippin,
Cox.

We could look it up, I said once,
on Google.
She gave me a pitying look,
like I was missing the point.

❧

Spring came in a riot of blossoms.
We watched the petals drift
down,
   down,
      down,
to gently kiss her eyelids
and tangle in her hair.

Talked about her work at the gallery
in town, and mine at the academy,
and all the far-off places
she couldn't wait to see:

Paris.
   Istanbul.
      Rome.

I'll take you, I said, and kissed
the cool surface of her wrist.
I promise.

❧

One for you, one for me,
and one for the apple tree man.
Once the first fruit bloomed
the rest came quickly.
They became pies and cordials
to share with my students,
pancakes on Sunday mornings,
mulled wine to stave the evening chill.

The scent of cinnamon and spice
clung and caught me unawares
in subtle sunkissed moments.
I'd remember her smile,
the soft murmur of her humming
as she cooked.

❧

After the accident,
the smell of cinnamon made me sick.

I returned to work quickly,
too quickly; too hard to stay at home
and watch the grass grow long,
the paint peel from the fence posts,
the bees press their furry faces
up against the window.

I snapped at my students.
I snapped at the parents.
I manufactured reasons
to work late, late into the night
so I wouldn't have to listen
to the silence as I fell asleep.

One evening I locked the gates
not long after sundown,
the sky streaked in gold,
the air with a richness
that reminded me of old days:
of cinnamon and wood smoke,
of cider on the air.

It was Halloween.
I hadn't even noticed.

Frail Little Embers

The house was dark and sightless,
the garden choked in thorns.
A breeze rustled, revealed

late this year, the colour of sunset
on new spring grass. A single apple
hanging at shoulder height, alone.

I grasped the fruit, watched its colours
play across its skin—rust and ochre
and scarlet and marigold.

It smelled of autumn sunsets,
fresh-cut grass and pastry dough,
cinnamon clinging to an old suit.

It smelled of long, dark lonely nights,
of drowning in memories
and waking to a nightmare.

I threw it hard against the trunk,
turned away and heard it break
somewhere in the dark,
   turned away and let the house
     devour me.

❧

Night came, uninvited,
filled the air
with laughing, shouting,

whistling, fireworks.
Trees creaked and groaned
like old men at a card table.

I put the kettle on and lay
across the sofa that became
bedroom, office,
refuge, world.
Every time I climbed the steps
to the room we shared, I thought

I could almost see her,
leaning out the window,
watching the apples turn red.

ಸ

The wind whistled
through a gap where the window
didn't quite pull shut all the way,
carrying scents of autumn, of cider,
old memories and new ones,
carrying shadows and moonlight
and lamplight, and for a moment—

    A figure stood beneath the apple tree.

But no—I was wrong.
It was only leaves and shadows
    after all.

I woke to stillness
and silence and sunrise
washing the curtains in rose.

To dew-strewn grass,
the mist of morning,
a man against the apple tree.

A face hidden by a battered straw hat;
a body all edges
and elbows
and knees.

The air had a touch of winter to it,
of dying things
and golden hours.
He greeted me with a tip of his hat.

Good morning, he said,
    and a happy All Hallows' to you.

I meant to say, *Who are you?* Instead:
    Halloween was yesterday.

Hallows' Eve, yes,
    This is Hallows' morning.

Apple Seeds

He played with something in his hand:
rust and ochre and scarlet and marigold.

Have you any cider?
    I told him that I didn't.

    Ah, well. Sit. Break Hallows' fast with me.

Now that I could see him well,
there was something in his look
perhaps I did know after all;
a memory from long ago.
A face dark with too much sun
and slashed deep with laughter.

I knew her when she was young, you know.
    The crisp morning air tasted harsh and metallic.
Back at the house in the old country.
There was an apple tree there too, a big one,
big enough to reach the sky,
big enough to hold the world.
And in the earth beside it was a dip
that became an ocean in the rain.
She'd sit beside it for hours and hours,
just waiting and watching. Used to think
she could see the future in it.

I pictured my wife from a few old photos,
jeans too short for her skinny legs,
plait running all down her back.
My throat tightened.

Frail Little Embers

She even saw you in it, once.

He looked at me for the first time, then,
a quick glance of beady black eyes.
Amused, perhaps a little sad.

Can't foresee everything,
   I guess.

❧

A knife stroke, a twist, three equal pieces.
   Cheers. Sláinte. À ta santé.
A hand dark and gnarled as an old tree root.
   Take the apple, it's tradition.

We shared the fruit, the man and I,
in dew-strewn grass and golden light.
Drank the warmth of summer,
the glow of evenings by the fire.
Flavours I had thought
I'd never taste again.

   One for you, one for me—

There's only two of us, I said.

He broke the third piece into two—
   Wrong.
—offered one to me.

Apple Seeds

She lives in you.
And in me. The wind, the light, these apple seeds.
Apple juice ran down his chin.
    She was a good neighbour, your lady.

I ate the final bite
and tasted home.

❦

In the grass, glowing in the morning light,
were three
shiny
brown
    apple seeds.

I gathered them carefully
and counted one by one:
Paris.
    Istanbul.
      Rome.

A bumblebee sat by the back door
in patient expectation.
It buzzed at me, and then took off
towards the open sky.

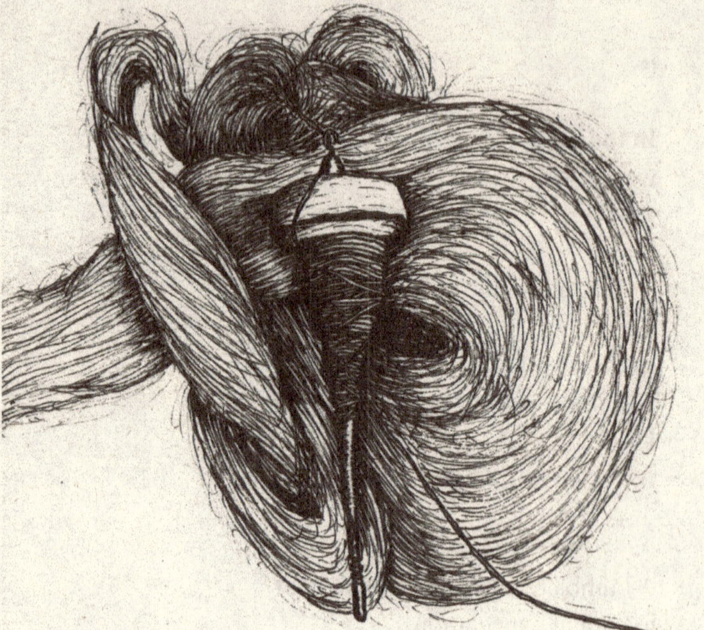

The Fleeting Ones

Clotho and Lachesis had a problem. Their sister was ill.

The women got ill very rarely, since they were cautious and never left their home, a cosy stone cottage at the foot of the river Lethe. It was happening to Atropos more and more though, her centuries sneaking up on her at last. The last time had been in 1912 after a sinking ship had nearly overwhelmed them, and Atropos had coughed for days, pulling her shawl tight around herself and cutting rough, uneven strokes with her shears.

Clotho knew that somewhere in the pile she wove, Atropos's thread was waiting.

She never halted in her spinning, but by unspoken agreement she and Lachesis fed the finished threads through a little slower, allowing Atropos to catch her breath as she hefted the shears in her mottled, shaking hands and cut the lives of those in the world of men. Clotho felt strange being the one to set the pace for the three of them. So often she turned to Lachesis to guide her rhythm, as she turned to her in so many things, and in some inexplicable way it felt as though their roles had been reversed. Atropos' decay left Lachesis cracked and vulnerable in a way that Clotho did not understand.

Slowing down gave her a chance to watch some of the lives glistening in the cloud-like fibre at her feet: a ballet dancer stubbornly taking the stage in spite of a damaged ankle; a young, promising athlete who had run off his bold mouth to a rival team member the night before; a widow who had just lost her husband and child in a car crash and was now staring down the edge of a grassy cliff at the hungry, merciful sea below. Even after so long, Clotho still ached at the beauty of each and every one of them. At the hopes, dreams, love, and—yes—even the pain, the storm of human feeling so perfect in its impermanent intensity that she could never have.

Atropos had shed such foolishness years ago, and Lachesis… well, it was difficult to say. Perhaps she remembered what it was like to yearn, even if she did so no longer. Clotho carefully fed her sister the twisted thread, watched her measure it by eye between her expert fingers.

With a hacking cough, Atropos gnashed at it with her shears. The thread went dark.

Clotho spun the spindle across her knees, watching the material catch and twist, gently teasing out the little snags of illness and heartbreak and loss. She wrapped the thread around the spindle shaft. It shimmered like sea spray under her fingers, and her breath caught.

Him.

She had watched him in her spinning for days, the young man with his fingers always covered in oil paint. His soul glowed brighter than any she had seen since that jazz musician, the Duke of something-or-other, nearly a century ago. She watched the way lines formed a focused H between his eyes as he concentrated on getting the blend of colours just right, and how the lines shifted to the outer corners of his eyes as he smiled, pleased with his work. She watched his strong, smooth hands pull out his finest brush and sign his name in the lower right corner of the canvas. His movements were so gentle, and yet Clotho imagined those hands capable of a great many things, gentle things and things where gentleness would be cast aside like the dead threads that Atropos cut.

Is this love? she wondered. Clotho had seen many, many loves, great ones and fleeting ones, not only in the world of men but in the world of gods and the seas and woodlands in which they roamed. But even as priestess, millennia ago, that love had been denied to her by her vows. When the sisters came to her and offered her a new path, she'd thought it a gift. She hadn't considered what she would be giving in return.

When Atropos' time came and Lachesis took up the shears, Clotho would learn the art of measuring thread while teaching another to take her place at the spindle. She caught herself wondering what might come if instead of taking one priestess from the temples, they found two. One to spin and one to measure. Their hands would be young, their hearts proud, and perhaps Lachesis would not need Clotho to stay—

Her sister nudged her gently with her shoulder, and Clotho realised she'd only wound the thread part way. She turned her eyes away in shame for her thoughts and twisted it slowly, maddeningly slowly, around the ancient wood. The man turned at his easel then and Clotho felt the whisper of his breath around her fingers. For an impossible moment it seemed as though he could sense her, feel her, that her breath touched him too.

She watched sidelong as Lachesis pulled the thread between her hands and examined it with a critical eye. It seemed so short. Surely there was more of his story yet to tell? And yet Lachesis was never wrong.

Atropos coughed again, and Clotho and Lachesis paused respectfully. This time, however, the coughing didn't stop—she clutched her chest and gasped for air. The shears clattered to the ground.

"Sister?" Lachesis said, alarmed.

Atropos fell to her knees, hiding her cough behind one hand and waving them away impatiently with the other. "Never mind," she said, in a voice like needles on glass. "Mind the thread."

Clotho and Lachesis looked down at the glistening thread in their hands. Clotho wondered if her sister could see how brightly it shone.

Lachesis turned to her. "You will have to cut it, Sister."

"Me?" Her mouth dropped open in shock.

"I cannot," she said, "I must hold it still. Hurry, the thread is growing slack."

Clotho stumbled to her feet and picked up Atropos's shears. They were heavier than they looked, and rust was beginning to spread from the join like a stain of blood. She looked back at the artist's thread and felt her heart break.

It slackened little by little, like aging skin. She wanted to tear it from her sister's grip and hold it close, guard it tight against her from the sorrows of the world, keep it safe even as its light withered away to nothing in her hands.

But would that be any life at all?

She met Lachesis's eyes and was surprised to find something like understanding in them.

"A life is not any dimmer for being fleeting," Lachesis said softly.

Clotho lifted the shears. As she turned back to the thread she was struck not by agony, as she expected, but by a sudden rush of gratitude. To have known him in some small way, to exist in a world where such light could flourish in the time it was given. And suddenly she understood that the love she felt for him, for her sisters, was so much bigger than any one life.

From watching Atropos she'd expected them to be dull and brittle, but they cut cleanly through the thread in an instant. It glowed like a fading ember as it drifted to the floor.

She picked it up and put it in the pocket of her dress.

Clotho helped Atropos to her feet. She felt the frail, bird-like bones in her grasp and wondered how long it would be until she fed her sister her own thread.

Atropos nodded gratefully, and Clotho went back to her spinning. The ballet dancer held a perfect *arabesque* to rapturous applause.

Perhaps her path had been a gift all along. To know that he had lived, felt sunlight, brought love and art into being. To stand witness to the heartbreaking beauty of simply being alive. Perhaps it could be enough.

She fed Lachesis the thread and watched each glowing, glorious spark of life pass through her fingers.

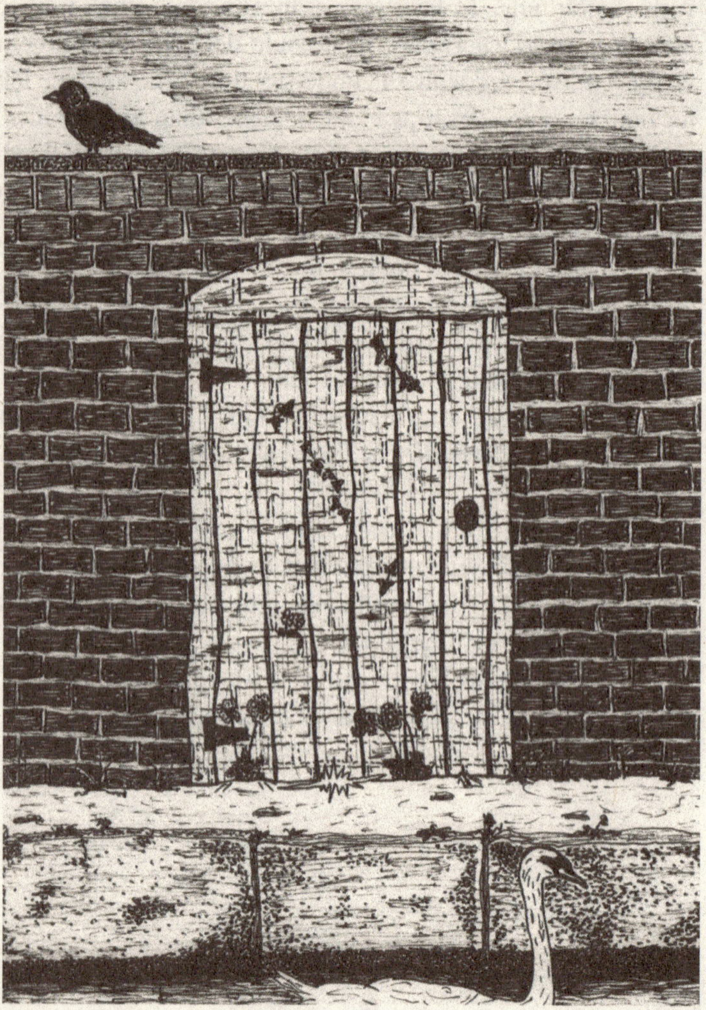

Songbird

With a brittle stick of willow charcoal, Wren sketched the swan that skimmed across the surface of the Grand Canal. Bold, simple strokes, using charcoal to fill in shadow and watching the swan come to life in the blank white space. The monochrome concision was a stark contrast to the riot of colour on the mural behind her.

She dipped her finger in the scummy canal water and smeared it onto the page beneath the swan's belly. It left a faint greenish tinge behind as it dried in the sun.

She had always loved their silent glide, the carefully restrained power in their imposing wings. *Mute swans*, they were called. Before he left, Wren's father once told her that when a swan was close to death, it keened the loveliest, most heartwrenching song. But it only ever sang it in private, because it didn't want to bring pain and grief to those it loved.

Wren's mother never liked that story.

Wren sat in front of the brightly painted mural every Wednesday after school, because that's when her mother had her group therapy and didn't come home until later. At night Wren would lie in bed and listen to her mother cry softly in the other room. She didn't think the group therapy was working.

She reached out and touched the drawing, careful not to smudge the kohl-black lines.

Swan. She formed the syllable in her mouth, shaped her lips around the letters. No sound came out. In thirteen years she'd never once heard the sound of her own voice, though sometimes she rolled the sounds around on her tongue, imagining what they would taste like.

Even having the word that close to her teeth gave her a lurching thrill, like standing on the edge of a precipice and realising if you took one more step you would fall a long, long way and it would hurt *a lot*.

She pressed her lips firmly together.

As the swan paddled onwards and away down the water, Wren turned to look at the wall. It stretched out in a vast panorama on either side, a nexus of colour against the grey Dublin landscape.

Images sprawled across it in a kind of beautiful chaos: a genie rising from a dusty old lamp; a white-tailed fox and a lady walking side by side; three little girls playing with witch hats and broomsticks. Wren was certain the mural shifted when no one was looking. Every time she sat down at the canal she discovered something new, and sometimes when she looked for an image she'd seen before, it was gone.

A gentle rain began to fall and the afternoon light melted across the water. Tourists and their selfie sticks faded into the mist. Wren closed her sketchbook with a wistful sigh, knowing that the next time she opened it the swan would be smudged beyond recognition. She put the book in her backpack and walked away from the painted wall, away from the canal, until she reached the weathered red-brick terrace house. It was divided into four apartments. The front door was painted a cheerful yellow, though the paint was beginning to crack in places.

Inside, the walls smelled of cigarettes and sticky-sharp red wine. Wren's mother sat at their table in a strappy dress that accentuated her sharp, angular shoulders. She'd never been a large woman, but Wren was sure her mother had become smaller than she once was, like a broken toy collapsing in on itself. Or maybe it was just that Wren was bigger now.

Did you eat? She formed the words with her fingers. Her mother glanced up and shook her head absently. Wren hesitated, unsure if she had actually registered the question. She crossed the hall to the table and picked up the ruled notepad she always kept by her chair.

Did you eat? She slid the notepad under her mother's eyes.

"Oh." Wren's mother seemed to shake herself awake. "No, I...no, not yet." She ran a hand through her matted hair, leaving more tangles than there'd been before. Wren's heart lurched, a feeling so familiar now that she seemed to live in it, of helplessness and shame and despair. She wanted to say something that would make her mother's pain go away. *I'm sorry I'm like this, I'm sorry I don't know how to help, I'm sorry I wasn't enough.* But she had never trusted words. They were powerful, worryingly so, but clumsy and blunt. It was too easy to stumble with them and break something.

There were no words that could fix this.

Wren went into the kitchen, which was really the same room but with tiles instead of carpet, and pulled out two tins of vegetable barley soup. She emptied them into a pan, heated the soup until it bubbled, and ladled it into two bowls. She brought them to the table one by one.

They sipped their soup in silence for a moment. It was the silence that made it all real, the blistering emptiness that clung to the walls like second-hand smoke. Before, Wren's mother was always singing, "Sentimental Journey" or "Summertime" or sometimes just humming with a dreamy smile on her face. Even when she was quiet, the afterimage of her voice seemed to hover in the air.

Wren's mother didn't sing anymore.

She looked up from the bowl and said, "How was school?"

Wren pulled the notepad over and hesitated. School didn't vary much. She ate her lunch alone out on the front lawn, or in the covered courtyard behind the building if it was raining. She didn't have any friends, but nobody was really mean to her, either. It was like if you didn't speak your mind out loud, if you didn't announce yourself every time you entered a room, you might as well not exist.

Except for a new teacher, Miss March, who was paying her more attention lately, asking if everything was alright at home. She even learned how to say hello in sign language, which Wren thought was a bit stupid because she could hear her say hello just fine, but she guessed the woman was just trying to make an effort. The teacher's blue eyes bored into her, as if Wren was a locked box that she was trying to jimmy open. She said she hoped Wren's mother would give her a call sometime.

Wren stared down at the notepad. How was she supposed to get all that across with twenty-six spindly little letters?

Instead she drew a picture of a telephone. Their red plastic one that said Coca-Cola on it.

"They want me to call?"

Wren nodded hesitantly.

"Okay." Her mother looked down at her soup, already receding back inside herself. Wren tore out the phone drawing and set it aside so her mother wouldn't forget. She finished her soup and went into the other room to do her homework.

When she came out later, her mother was asleep on the sofa and the soup was cold on the table, the barley all congealed together. Wren brought it back to the kitchen and silently poured it down the drain.

※

She returned to the canal walk the next afternoon, even though it wasn't Wednesday yet. She'd been avoiding Miss March's gaze all day. The teacher was nice, letting Wren do some of her homework in pictures instead of words, but Wren didn't know how to answer the questions she saw dancing in the woman's eyes. How could she explain that her mother was broken, and it was all her fault?

She meandered along the familiar path, the murky canal water on one side and the jewel-toned mural on the other. The genie had disappeared. The lamp remained, knocked on its side and forgotten. She passed other images, familiar faces she saw every week: a dancing couple wearing masquerade masks, his black and hers white; six swans circling a burning building; an old, old woman in a red hooded cloak with a wolf lying by her side. For a moment, in the shifting light off the water, the wolf appeared to meet Wren's eyes. But no—he was looking at the elderly lady, with the tired camaraderie of very old friends.

Past them was something she hadn't seen before, though she must have walked by it a thousand times. Its sunbleached colours looked like they had been there longer than any of the others. It was a picture of a wooden door set into a brick wall, like the ones that lined the back alleys behind some of the old houses. Delicately painted ivy leaves and blushing herb robert blossoms peeked out of the brickwork. A row of poppies ran along the bottom edge and seemed to sway in the wind.

It looked just like a real door. Wren ran her fingers over it to be sure, but all she felt were brush strokes over the cool surface of the cement. She kneeled down and touched the scarlet flowers.

Poppies, she thought, and wrinkled her nose. She disliked the hard Ps, like bubbles bursting on the tongue one after the other. Why did people always feel the need to name everything? The flowers were beautiful just the way they were.

She was about to stand up when she noticed something. Right where the fake door met the fake bricks, a gentle current of air wafted towards her from the other side.

Wren knew it wasn't real, but she couldn't help wondering where it might lead. Narnia? A car park? She ran her finger along the join.

A splash and a scream made her jump. She turned around. Some dumb tourists were feeding bread to a swan, and the bird had jumped onto the bank with a flutter of its enormous wings. The scream turned into embarrassed laughter. The swan poked at the grass, unbothered.

Wren glanced back at the door, then continued along the path. She didn't have time to spend looking at pictures today.

There was a phone box at one end of the canal, just before the little footbridge and just past the square where kids from Wren's school sometimes took their skateboards. She ducked inside and pulled the phone off the hook. It was heavier than the Coca Cola one.

She dug out a scrap of paper, mangled from months in her pocket, and pushed the buttons on the phone's number pad. Her hands shook.

He answered on the fourth ring.

"Hello?"

Wren stopped breathing.

"Hello," he said again, "is anyone there?" They were both silent for a moment, and then her father let out a loud breath. "Wren, is that you?"

She nodded, even though he couldn't see her.

"I miss you, sweetie." His voice sounded hoarse, like he hadn't used it in a while. It wasn't like she remembered it. How much could someone's voice change in only a few months?

Please come home, Wren thought. If only she could say the words out loud. She wanted to say them so badly the day he stood in their hallway in front of her, a suitcase at his feet. *Please stay*. Instead she just stared, blinking away tears of confusion. Though deep down, a part of her understood. What kind of man would want a daughter who had never even said "I love you"?

Her father spoke again into the phone. "I don't think we should talk for a while, Wren."

Please come home. She began forming the words with her fingers, but one of her hands had a phone in it, so she couldn't do it right. *Please*.

She shaped the sound in her mouth. *Please*. A sharp bubble on the tongue, like *poppies*.

"Take good care of your mam, will you?" her father said. He already sounded so far away.

Just one tiny word.

"I love you."

"Pl—"

He hung up.

Wren lowered the plastic phone and stared at it, gripping it so hard she thought her fingers would break.

~·~

She dragged her feet up the steps to the townhouse, dreading the silence and cigarette smoke and suffocating weight of her failure. It had been a long shot. She knew, since that moment in the hallway five months ago, that he wasn't coming back. She just didn't know what else to do.

Her mother was asleep on the sofa when she arrived. Wren watched her for a moment, wondering when she'd last gone to work. She looked both older and younger than she remembered, withered and brittle-boned yet vulnerable as a child. Wren wondered if she found some peace when she slept, wherever she was.

She pulled the ratty blanket off the back of the sofa and laid it over her mother's body. Then she went into the bathroom and stared at her face in the mirror. She stuck out her tongue and examined it. It didn't look any different from anybody else's tongue.

She looked down and noticed a smear of red against the white porcelain. Wren stared at it for a moment, unable to process what she was seeing. As the truth took shape, she shuffled through explanations in her mind. Her mother had cut herself shaving. She'd torn off a hangnail. She'd dropped one of her expensive lotions and cut herself on the glass.

Feeling strangely disconnected, Wren inched back into the living room. Her mother shifted but didn't wake. Wren lifted a corner of the blanket and saw the cotton bandage wrapped around her mother's arm. The edges had dried sepia brown.

She stumbled into a sitting position at her mother's side.

I don't know how to help, she thought. *I don't know what to do.* Find someone to call a doctor? Go to school and ask Miss March? She needed a grownup. Except a grownup might want to take her mother away, and then she'd have no one. She would be all alone.

Wren watched her mother's slow, even breathing. With her finger, she traced images into the carpet. The three of them together, as a family. Poppies. A door.

She didn't go to school the next day, afraid of what would happen if her mother was by herself. Instead she sat on the floor and drew with her willow sticks—sharp, bold, angry lines in rapid succession, turning pages in the sketchbook as she poured out her despair and her rage.

She reached the back cover of the book and was momentarily disoriented, as though caught between dreaming and waking. Two of her charcoal sticks had snapped; she hadn't even noticed. She stood up, her legs stiff, and set her sketchbook aside. Her stomach rumbled. She made sandwiches and gave one to her mother, who was sitting by the window and watching the leafy street below.

After she'd eaten, Wren opened the sketchbook.

Some of the images had smudged so badly they were unrecognisable, just angry storms of lines and curves and shadows. On other pages she found her mother and father, smiling at each other and holding hands.

And doors.

The same door, the one painted on the wall at the canal, over and over again. She touched one of them cautiously, felt the charcoal smudge beneath her fingers. It gave her a funny feeling in her chest that reminded her of shaping words in her mouth—a rush of vertigo, of standing at the edge of a precipice she couldn't come back from.

She gathered her book and her charcoal and stuffed them into her school bag. Then she went over to her mother. The sandwich lay half eaten at her side.

Come, Wren said with her hands.

Her mother frowned and stood sluggishly. "What's wrong?"

Wren didn't answer. An idea was forming in her head, though she was afraid to look at it too closely in case it shattered. Her mother let her pull them both to the coat stand, the door. As an afterthought, Wren wrapped the sandwich half and stuffed it in her bag with her sketchbook. If she was right, they might not be coming home for a long time.

She led her mother along the road to the canal, past the footbridge and the empty square and the phone box. They'd walked along the canal when she was younger, the three of them, watching the swans cut roads into the water that faded again in their wake.

The door would be near the end of the mural, just beyond the phone box. But a moment later she stumbled to a halt.

The mural was gone.

At first she couldn't understand what she was looking at. Everything had the same shape and angles it always had. But along the wall, stretching off into the distance, all she could see was white.

Wren gripped her mother's hand like she was a child. She couldn't breathe. She felt as though she'd finally stumbled over the precipice and couldn't stop falling.

They reached the wall and Wren touched it with her fingertips. It was tacky, but no longer wet, even though a piece of paper stuck to it said 'Wet Paint'. Another one said 'Dublin City Council Site Notice'. Wren tried to read the tiny words below, but her vision blurred.

"They're building a hotel," her mother said, skimming the notice. She looked at Wren. "We used to—" but she broke off, biting her lip.

Wren nodded and signed, *I remember*.

They sat down in the grass. The fresh white paint reflected the grey sky and the light off the water, making everything brighter, like an overexposed photograph. Wren leaned her head against the cool cement, not even caring that the paint made her hair sticky. Her mother leaned her head against the wall too, and they sat like that together. The fresh air lightened her mother's eyes and brought a little bit of colour into her face. She gave Wren a small smile.

Wren touched the wall again. It looked like a blank page from her sketchbook, stretching out in all directions without end. She dug out her willow charcoal. The rain would wash it away before long; rain was never far away in Dublin.

She drew a careful, cautious line, stark stormy black against endless white. When nothing happened, she added another line, and then another, until a tree bloomed out of the emptiness. She drew the eyes and flaking white bark of a bare birch in winter. Her mother watched the tree take shape.

"You've got better," she said, as if she wasn't quite expecting this. Wren smiled shyly and handed the willow stick to her mother.

She shook her head. "I've never had a head for drawing. You get that from your—" She stopped, and some of the light went from her eyes.

Wren carefully picked up her mother's hand and wrapped it around the charcoal. It felt like holding a baby bird, brittle and delicate, as if one quick movement might break it. She pulled her mother's hand forward until the charcoal touched the blank surface of the wall. She let her own hands fall and waited.

Her mother adjusted her grip and slowly drew the outline of a crow, the grey ones that often gathered under the footbridge. The lines were shaky, like a child's, but a soft smile blossomed across her face.

Wren took out another stick and drew a magpie beside the crow, and a Tayto wrapper in the magpie's mouth. The magpie was offering it to the crow as a gift. Her mother laughed, then clapped a hand over her mouth, the sound startling after months and months of silence.

Wren kept drawing. She felt the unsteady stroke of her mother's hand beside hers, and together they drew the footbridge across the canal, the rooftops above them, a bench on the pathway, a riverboat. The wind murmured in the grass, and beneath, so faint she almost missed it, the soft sound of humming. It was "Summertime".

She added a row of poppies beneath the bench, and ripples under the riverboat. They sat comfortably together, side by side, as a new world of light and shadow emerged ahead of them.

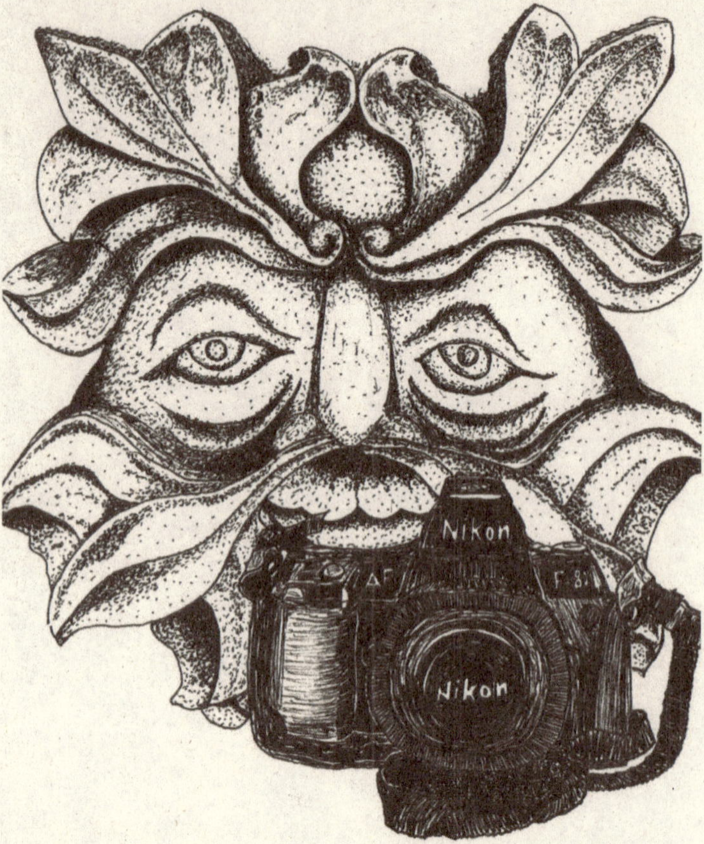
Nikon
Nikon

One Hundred Words for Loss

The trick, Liam's father had said, *is finding beauty in things that other people miss*. The last rays of sunset glinting off a wrought-iron balcony. The gentle curl of a fallen leaf against a brick road. An abandoned table on a café terrace, espresso cups and lipstick stains carefully preserved in time. Tiny little sparks of life beneath the gritty grey filter of the world.

Diana, Liam's girlfriend, had been like that too. She saw vibrancy in everything, from crumpled Coke cans glittering in the rain to architectural motifs hidden around decaying doors. That's how Liam started seeing the Green Men.

Diana found the first one above the door to the church in Hampstead where his father's funeral was being held. They'd never met, she and Liam's father—he kept putting it off, and then a year had gone by, and then it was very suddenly too late. His father would have liked her.

She was wearing a black velvet dress with some lace thing at the throat that set off her fox-red hair, and Liam wore an off-the-rack suit that didn't fit him properly. He'd brought his camera with him, a clunky old Nikon DSLR that had been a gift from his father, though apart from the odd birthday gathering it sat in a cupboard and was never used. It hung around his neck from a thick strap, its weight suffocating and comforting at the same time.

The procession filed out, aunts and cousins twice removed who Liam had only met in passing, murmuring things like *So sad, and so much life ahead of him. He always was a bit odd, wasn't he? Wonder what time the pubs close.*

Diana squeezed his hand and pointed back towards the church. They stopped, and the aunts and cousins parted around them like a sluggish sea.

A leafy face peered at them from above the door. Its stubby nose was eroded with time and its sightless stone eyes were crinkled in laughter.

"Wonder what he's got to be so pleased about," Liam said.

Diana took both of his hands in hers. "He's smiling because he knows your father's going to be alright," she said. "And he's proud of you."

Liam looked at his feet. "And how would old Leafy up there know that?"

She looked at him with mock severity. "Green Men know all kinds of things. You could do worse than listen to one of them."

"I suppose I could." He filled with gratitude for her, this woman who saw such extraordinary things in such a decrepit world, who came with him to a funeral for a man she'd never even known. Diana took his arm and they followed his relatives towards the gate. Just before they reached it, Liam turned back and snapped a picture of the Green Man.

After that he began to see them everywhere. Around the old churches that dotted the city. Carved into gates that edged the parks. Old houses. Pavements. Above the entrance to a tube station. All of these laughing, scowling, pensive faces that he'd never taken the time to notice because he couldn't see the world the way Diana and his father could.

He began taking photos.

He brought a new lens for closeups and another for the ones high up on buildings, and scoured London for Green Men hidden in the city's bones. Through the eye of the camera he learned to see the contrast of light and shadow in a way he never had before, the juxtaposition of soft edges and sharp ones, the way the city's secrets glimmered just beneath the surface, waiting to be carved out. Liam had an idea that he'd put them all into a keepsake coffee-table book for Diana and give it to her for her birthday. She loved things like that, myths and nature spirits and old stories.

The book turned out great—better than he'd expected. Each face was unique, bathed in the golden light of sunset or the rosy wash of morning or slicked black with rain. He arranged them by neighbourhood under headings like *Hampstead, Highgate, Knightsbridge, Earl's Court*, and paid extra for the "Professional" option with glossy paper and faux-leather covers.

By the time the finished book arrived in the post, Diana was already gone.

She left most of her stuff behind. She'd taken her shoes, though, and an amber necklace she loved to wear, and her sketchbook. In its place was a note that said, *I'm sorry. I love you*.

Her work called. So did her parents, and her friends, and finally the police. Liam said *I don't know* so many times that the words began to bleed together, and he stopped answering the phone. He threw the Green Man book across the room. Then he went over and picked it up, and put it in a drawer with some of Diana's clothes. He put the camera away too.

The next day he came across a photography contest advertised by the BBC. He paid the admission fee, sent them his digital file for the Green Man book, and promptly forgot about it. With Diana and his father both gone, the world faded back into the shades of grey it had always been.

A few months later the network wrote to tell him he'd won. The prize was quite a lot of money and a feature on the BBC website, and a publishing deal. *Green Men of London* sold surprisingly well, and Liam kept hoping that Diana would somehow see it, wherever she was, and come home.

The publisher asked him what he was working on next.

Autumn slipped seamlessly into winter, as it so often did in London, the colour slowly bleaching away until you woke one morning and realised it had already been winter for weeks.

One November morning Liam woke to frost on the windowpane, and a faint grey mist of snow that spun lazily over the rooftops and never seemed to reach the ground. He was reminded of a day he and Diana had gone to watch carollers in St James's Park during a rare snowfall.

Do you know that Inuit people have one hundred words for snow? she'd said. Liam said no, he hadn't known. She reached up and caught a snowflake on her gloved fingertip. They leaned over it, holding their breath so it wouldn't melt, and examined its perfect crystalline facets. The heat drifted off their bodies and they watched the tiny snowflake slip away into nothingness.

Liam wrote back and told the publisher his next book would be called *One Hundred Words for Frost*.

He bought a new macro lens that cost more than the camera so he could capture the delicate hoarfrost on the edges of ivy leaves, the thorn-like rime blooming across crumpled crisps packets discarded in the street, the swirls of fernfrost unfurling across café windows, capture them so they couldn't slip away from him between one breath and the next. Up close, he was amazed at how varied it all was. There was a multifaceted, minuscule world that he'd never opened his eyes to. He'd never known how.

Liam explored the dregs of alleyways, the forgotten places. He kept feeling like if he turned one more corner he might find her, waiting to show him a tiny piece of the world she had found.

He turned onto a street he didn't recognise and came to one of the city's many green spaces, a docile park fenced in by cast iron gates and veined in meandering pathways. At this time of year the grass was coarse and dry; the paths were stripped of tourists, and the small pond encased by a glassy membrane of ice. A family of ducks huddled together on the bank for warmth.

Farther in, a crumbling stone wall rose sluggishly out of the ground and made it about three metres before giving up. Some old fort that had been left behind to attract the tourists, or for a couple to steal a kiss behind. Liam recognised it now; Diana had taken him to an exhibition here during the summer, some friend of hers, or a friend of a friend, had displayed some paintings, leaning them up against this wall. There'd been a feature about it in *Metro*. There was, if he remembered correctly, an underground station just at the other end.

He went up to the wall and inspected it for potential images. An old spider's web clung to an even older crevice, laden with globules of ice. Liam snapped a photo before going around to the other side of the wall. It was only about four metres wide. He ran his fingers over the edges of the stones and watched his breath come out of him in bursts of mist.

He was just taking a step back and raising his camera when he saw it—a contorted stone face peering through carved holly leaves on one of the lowermost stones. Liam had to kneel down to look at it. It reminded him of one from *Green Men* that he'd found embedded in the pavement, probably recycled from some long-fallen fortress. He must have stepped over it a thousand times.

This one was caked in dirt and mulch clumped together by frost. He gently pushed the debris away. Its sightless eyes were crinkled in laughter. It wouldn't go in the book, the new one, but Liam took a photo of it anyway. He wished he could show Diana.

He stood and turned away from the wall. Even in his thick gloves, his fingers were growing frigid.

A snowflake drifted onto his hand.

Boots crunching on brittle leaves, Liam made his way across the park to the train that would take him home. He was getting ready to commit several atrocities to the first cup of tea that crossed his path. More snowflakes spiralled out of the air, dimming the city noise.

The trees at this end were bigger, heavy oaks and beeches clinging to remnants of autumn, dead leaves shuddering like old bones against the pale branches. The pavement tapered off into dry earth and up ahead, a red fox scurried through the undergrowth. Liam stopped, suddenly unsure of his direction. He'd been certain the park was smaller than this.

He turned, wondering if he should retrace his steps, but the path he'd taken was buried in snow. Trees thrust up into the sky, great timeless things, the beeches and oaks sheltered by cedars and redwoods. The first stirrings of primordial fear flickered to life.

Then Liam saw her.

Diana was sitting on a torn tree stump the size of an SUV. Her hair was matted with leaves and briars. He wondered if he was truly seeing her, more out of loyalty to his sanity than anything else, but then she looked up, and her face split into a big smile, and all his intruding doubts fell away.

She slipped off the tree stump and came over to him. He suddenly felt as shy as the day they met. Snow clung to his nose, his arms, his hair, snow like they almost never saw in London, and he realised there was no snow on Diana anywhere, and then her arms were around him, and her body was warm, and nothing more mattered at all.

"I was right, you know," she muttered into his chest.

"About what?" His words drifted away into the snow.

"Your father. He is proud of you."

Liam pulled away and looked at her. His body stung in the sudden chill. "Are you…?" He couldn't bring himself to say it. It was funny, he thought, how it had never once occurred to him that Diana might be dead. Even when it began to seem like the most likely option, he knew she wasn't. He would have felt it.

She shook her head. "No. No, I'm…somewhere else. But I saw him. He's a really lovely man. We had a nice long chat about yarrow and art."

Liam started to smile, then had a sharp, uncomfortable thought. "Am I?"

"I don't think so." She bit her lip, white teeth on red skin. "I'm not sure why you're here. I suppose it's because now you can see. I mean, the way I can."

"And my father." It wasn't a question. His father and Diana were even more alike than Liam had thought.

"He told me he used to come here when he was alive. He was one of the lucky ones. Most of us don't get to choose." She smiled sadly. "He chose you."

But not you, Liam thought. *You didn't choose me.* Then he felt guilty for thinking it. She belonged here. He could see it in the glow of her eyes, in the soft movements of her bare feet against the snow-dusted ground, in the wild autumn-leaf tangle of her hair. Diana had become a Green Woman. Maybe she always had been, and he was just seeing it for the first time.

Diana took his hands in hers. She was so warm. "Liam, you're freezing."

"Am I?" The words came out in a chatter.

She leaned up and kissed his cheek. "You need to go, my love."

"But what about you?"

Diana shook her head. "It was never my home. Not the way it can be for you. Don't let seeing the world for what it really is keep you from living in it."

She kissed him again, on his lips, but this time she wasn't warm—she was ice-cold and feather-light, and his eyes fluttered closed, even though he knew she wouldn't still be there when he opened them again. That he was about to lose her one more time.

That he was saying goodbye.

The wind howled around him. Slowly, grudgingly, he opened his eyes.

Tiny wet snowflakes littered the air, turning wetter and gaining speed as they fell. A concrete path ran under his feet. It sloped gently towards a black gate, and from just beyond came the familiar rush of buses.

As he reached the gate, he turned back to look at the park. It was sparse and manicured and could have been any one of a hundred such green spaces peppering the city streets. And yet, every inch of it was alive with life and possibility. The knotted eyes peering out of a young birch tree. The fox that watched him from behind the crumbling stone wall before disappearing out of sight. Tiny little sparks of life beneath the gritty grey filter of the world.

Victoria Murphy M.D.
Licensed Bibliotherapist
A Little Princess

The Story Doctor

People went to the shiny, cut-glass medical clinic on Kingston Street when they were sick in their bodies. They came to Dr Murphy's back garden when they were sick in their hearts.

Victoria Murphy's practice looked nothing like the medical clinic on Kingston Street. Hers was in a repurposed garden shed with a thatched roof and yellow roses growing up one side of the door. On the other side, a brass plaque said:

Victoria Murphy, M.D.
Licensed Bibliotherapist

Dr Murphy unlocked the garden shed a few minutes before Mr Fitzpatrick, one of her regular patients, arrived. She always tried to arrive early and have a hot cup of tea at the ready. Her clinic had no sink or kitchen, but there was an electric hob and a kettle and a small shelf with mismatched teacups hanging from it, two cosy armchairs, and a tiny tea-stained table often crowded with books.

The kettle whistled just as Mr Fitzpatrick, a broad-shouldered man who taught at the local high school, arrived in a foul mood. His daughter, he explained, as Dr Murphy poured hot water into a chipped enamel teapot, his daughter Fiona, who sat in his class, had just had her heart broken by a testosterone-fuelled lout—who also sat in his class. Mr Fitzpatrick heard Fiona crying in her room each night, and then they both went to school in the morning and Mr Fitzpatrick had to restrain himself from striding across the classroom and putting the offending lout through a window.

Dr Murphy nodded sympathetically, biting back a smile at the thought of the man who handled her china teacups with such care putting anyone through a window. Yes, she agreed, first heartbreaks were hard. She took out her notebook and, holding it up close to her face, wrote out two prescriptions in big, careful letters.

Name: Stephen Fitzpatrick
The Twelve Lives of Samuel Hawley, by Hannah Tinti
Take one page with breakfast, Monday - Friday

Name: Fiona Fitzpatrick
Stargirl, by Jerry Spinelli
Take one chapter at bedtime 3-4x / week

Mr Fitzpatrick took the slips of paper and held them as carefully as if they were moths' wings.

After Mr Fitzpatrick let himself out, Dr Murphy looked at her notes. Her next appointment was someone new, Natalia Markova. When Natalia, a dark-haired woman in her early twenties, arrived, she greeted Dr Murphy in a heavy Russian accent and looked around the garden shed with naked curiosity. Dr Murphy offered Natalia a fresh pot of tea, but the woman shook her head and squeezed her fingers tight in front of her. They settled into the armchairs.

The Story Doctor

"So, what is troubling you, Natalia?"

The woman spoke into her lap. "When I come here three months ago, I join a group of women to make friends. Like me, they come from other places—India, China, Romania, America. It is not so…" She paused, thinking. "…frightening to be here."

"Yes," agreed Dr Murphy. "It is difficult to be somewhere new."

Natalia nodded emphatically. "But now they tell me I cannot come with them anymore, because I am Russian. Because my country is…" She frowned, again searching for words. "Not a good place." She looked up at Dr Murphy for the first time. "But I do nothing wrong! I do not take my guns and my bombs to other people's homes. I am trying to build again in a new way! Why blame me for my country's leaders?"

"I understand," said Dr Murphy. "Sometimes when people feel powerless to help, they try to help in the wrong ways. They blame, because to blame is to make sense of the senseless."

Some of the tension went from Natalia's shoulders. "Yes," she said, "it is like this."

"Would you like that tea now?" Dr Murphy asked.

She nodded slowly. "Thank you."

The steam drifted up like little ghosts, caught in the sunlight falling through the single window. When she was seated again, Dr Murphy took out her notebook and considered. Sometimes she had to dig deep into old memories to find the perfect book for a client; other times it appeared to her as though summoned, vibrant and filled with longing, like one broken half of a whole. Natalia's book danced behind her eyes.

"What day would you usually meet them?"

"Every Thursday."

Dr Murphy wrote out the prescription and handed it to her.

Name: Natalia Markova
You Bring the Distant Near, by Mitali Perkins
Take one chapter each Thursday at bedtime, and as needed.

Natalia accepted the piece of paper reverently. "Thank you, Dr Murphy. I am told that you make miracles happen. I am happy to begin reading my new book."

Dr Murphy smiled sadly. "I don't make miracles, Natalia. It's these men and women, these storytellers, who create the real magic. They heal us with entire worlds." She opened the door, letting in a wash of sunshine. "I hope you find everything here you are looking for."

Natalia left, and Dr Murphy poured the rest of the tea out into the garden. Her third appointment was Mrs Haverton, whose husband owned the pharmacy just down the road from the medical clinic on Kingston street. Mrs Haverton was always a little embarrassed to be in Dr Murphy's clinic, as though she was being disloyal to the chemicals and medications her husband packaged with such care. *But*, she'd admitted with a wistful sigh, *I always did love to read.*

Today Dr Murphy took one look at her and put the kettle back on.

Mrs Haverton's eyes were red from crying, and she moved with the slow, sludgy movements of someone much older. Dr Murphy helped her into one of the chairs.

"Now, Mrs Haverton," said Dr Murphy gently, as they waited for the water to boil, "why don't you tell me what's troubling you?"

The Story Doctor

"Well," she sniffed, "Dr Murphy." She toyed with a piece of tissue in her hands, scrunching it and smoothing it and crumpling it again. "It's my brother."

Dr Murphy took a breath and stood, adjusting the kettle on the heat so Mrs Haverton wouldn't see her expression. Having a constant rotation of tea on the go meant there was always something to do with her hands, somewhere to be when she needed to catch a moment's respite. Mrs Haverton's younger brother Geoffrey was always in some sort of trouble or another, swilling all his money away at the casino or being brought into Mr and Mrs Haverton's late at night by an apologetic policeman, who would mumble something about locking him up for disorderly conduct but never did. In the rare weeks when her brother was doing alright, Mrs Haverton had told her, he would apologise and give them a little money. They never asked him where he got it.

"How is Geoffrey doing?" Dr Murphy asked lightly, already considering and discarding titles in her head.

"Not very well, I'm afraid," said Mrs Haverton in a small voice. Dr Murphy returned with two teacups. She handed one to Mrs Haverton and sat down.

"He's just been to the clinic, you see," she went on. "On Kingston Street. He's been bellyaching about his stomach for ages, and I kept telling him to go, but he wouldn't hear of it, and then it got too bad, so finally…" She closed her eyes and clenched the tissue tight in her hand. "It's cancer. The doctors said if he'd gone to them sooner they might have been able to do something, but…but…he'll be lucky if he gets a few months."

Mrs Haverton dropped the tissue and wrapped her arms around herself. "I just thought…I mean, my husband's given him something for the pain, but I thought if you knew anything that might make the days a little easier…"

"Of course," Dr Murphy said softly. "I'm so sorry, Mrs Haverton. Your brother's a good man." The lie stung her lips on its way out, but it was the right thing to say. Mrs Haverton smiled, her eyes bright.

"He is, isn't he? He does try, you know. Not everybody sees that."

Dr Murphy took out her notebook and considered. Frayed family ties, the healing power of tragedy, the art of channelling despair into mindful living, stories about hope, stories about redemption, stories about survival, *The Salt House*, *The Fault in Our Stars*…

As she shuffled through books in her mind, one flashed in front of her eyes, vivid and insistent as a beacon. She hesitated a moment before turning to a new page.

"It's 'Lawlins', isn't it?" Dr Murphy asked.

Mrs Haverton looked up. "Yes, that's right."

Dr Murphy wrote out two prescriptions.

Name: Felicity Haverton
Napkin Notes, by Garth Callaghan
Take one chapter each evening between 6 and 9pm

Name: Geoffrey Lawlins
Touching the Void, by Joe Simpson
Take ~500 words daily before bed

She handed Mrs Haverton the scraps of paper, and the book in her mind faded away. "Please do make sure he reads it,

Mrs Haverton. Whatever it takes. Even just a few words, if that's all he can manage."

Mrs Haverton nodded. "Thank you, Dr Murphy."

She let herself out of the garden shed. Bright sunlight streamed in and hovered across the room for a moment; then the door closed again, and it was gone. The empty teacups lay abandoned on the table.

Once the woman had left, Victoria Murphy closed her eyes in the dimness for a moment's rest. Then she locked the shed and crossed the garden to the main house. It was too big for her, really, left to her by parents who expected her to fill it with another generation of Murphys. She felt more at ease in her clinic, which was barely large enough to seat two. It was difficult to walk through the halls of her house with their rows upon rows of books. Her parents had both been voracious readers, and every birthday and Christmas had meant something new to read in the warm glow of the fireplace, new spines to glisten and glimmer cheerfully from the walls of her room. The three of them would curl up in bed together and read *The Velveteen Rabbit* and *Madeline*, and later, *Inkheart* and *The Wizard of Oz*.

Now, as she ran a finger along the familiar leather bindings, it felt as though she were on a moving train and calling to a friend outside the window who couldn't quite hear her, close enough to touch but worlds and worlds away.

Victoria had lunch in the breakfast nook just off the kitchen, enjoying the warm sun against her bare shoulders. Then she went into the sitting room, sat on the ragged old sofa, and took out the eye drops she'd been given by the nice doctor at the clinic on Kingston Street.

The best we can hope for now, he had said, *is to slow it down.*

She carefully measured out two drops into the underlid of each eye, shut her eyes tight, and swished them around behind her eyelids. Then, keeping them firmly closed, she lay down on the sofa and slowly counted to one hundred and twenty.

Victoria Murphy had no appointments the next morning. Instead she put on a cheery yellow dress, pulled on a smart wool jacket, and went up the road to the medical clinic on Kingston Street.

The day was grey and dreary, and for that Victoria was grateful. The doctor had given her sunglasses to protect against the glare, but she disliked wearing them; they kept the world at a distance, filtering it into shades of sepia. But she kept them in her pocket, just in case.

The clinic was spacious and made up of trim, ninety-degree angles. Everything was white or grey except for the modernist abstract paintings on the wall, washed in calming shades of green and blue. Dr Blythe met her in the reception area with a smile. Victoria followed him into the examination room.

"How are you feeling today, Miss Murphy?" he said.

She hesitated. In spite of all the problems her clients heaped on her, she always felt uneasy talking about her own. But there was nothing to be gained by being dishonest with Dr Blythe, who had become, if not quite a friend, someone she could talk to. Someone who would examine each of her eyes with crystalline precision and never judge her or pity her for the despair he found in them.

"The headaches are worse," she admitted. "Everything is always so bright, except for…except for the edges." Dr Blythe knew that already. Her peripheral vision was closing in just a tiny bit more every day, the shadows that ringed her line of sight growing darker and darker, slowly devouring the world before her very eyes. For once, words couldn't save her.

Victoria knew what her book would be: Frances Hodgson Burnett's *A Little Princess*, where imagination and kindness were more powerful than the harsh realities of the world. She had a beautiful old clothbound copy her father used to read to her after her mother fell ill. His voice created a world for just the two of them, a safe place where she could forget for a few minutes at a time.

The book called out to her, pulsing insistently behind her eyes, but every time she pulled it down and opened it the words melted together, the edges too dark and everything else too bright, and a sharp pain lanced through her skull until she closed it again.

And so she left the book on the shelf, untouched, and every day was a little bit dimmer than the one before.

Dr Blythe invited her to come and sit at the retinal scanner. She balanced her chin on the leather strap and her arms on the metal bars on either side. With a whirr, a metal box with a pair of inset lenses rumbled up to her face. Though she was used to the sensation by now, she still tensed as the cold glass pushed up against her eyes.

Distantly, she heard the clattering of keys at Dr Blythe's computer. A red pinprick of light appeared in the distance in front of Victoria's eyes; it was painfully bright against the darkness.

"Are you taking the eye drops I gave you?"

Victoria looked away from the machine, rubbing her watery eyes. "Yes, every day."

Dr Blythe was frowning. He leaned towards the computer screen. Victoria couldn't see what he was looking at.

"Could we try once more, Miss Murphy?"

Something about his frown tugged at her, but she turned back to the lenses and forced her attention onto the red light. It wavered in and out of focus as she stared at it.

"Thank you."

She pulled away, closing her eyes to give them a moment's rest. A chair scraped as he sat down across from her.

There was silence. Victoria opened her eyes and focused them on his face. The rest of the office faded into shadow. The world was so small.

Dr Blythe took a deep breath. "It looks like your retina's deteriorating a bit faster than expected."

"Oh?" Victoria fought to keep her voice steady. "A bit? How much of a bit?"

He hesitated and looked down at his hands. Victoria looked at them too. They were rough hands, calloused and landscaped in tiny scars. "You may have…months. Maybe weeks."

"*Weeks?!*" Her voice jumped into a register she didn't know she had. "But you said two years. Just a few months ago, you told me I had two more years. I was going to…" What, exactly? Victoria had made and discarded plans like confetti, caught between her desire to see as much of the world as she could and her fear that it was already too late. She'd booked a flight to India, then cancelled it, terrified of wandering around half blind in a foreign country alone. She'd looked into classes in oil painting at the community college before realising that even writing out her prescriptions took more out of her than she liked to admit. The world was leaving her behind, and all she could do was sit and watch it disappear and recommend books she couldn't read and pretend they made any difference at all.

Dr Blythe finally met her eyes. "I'm so sorry, Victoria."

She suddenly felt stupid in her sunny yellow dress. She picked up her handbag and left the clinic, walking into two doorframes on her way out.

The weekend rolled by in an indecisive blur of wan sunlight and half-hearted storm clouds. Victoria walked through the garden that sprawled between the house and the shed, counting paces as she went. Sixteen paces from one door to the other. Four steps down from the house; four steps up to go back in again.

In between them, the garden was beginning to wake for summer. Yellowed winter grass shed in favour of verdant summer clothes; pale pink blossoms peeked out from the patch of wild strawberries and fluttered amidst the branches of the apple tree. Victoria touched every one, marvelling at the synaesthetic harmony of texture and colour, the two so perfectly intertwined that she couldn't tell where sight ended and touch began. The world was so beautiful it hurt.

Her book flashed behind her eyes again. *A Little Princess. Frances Hodgson Burnett. One chapter per day, on waking.* It was close enough that she could almost feel the cloth against her fingertips, but she knew the words were out of reach forever. She had even tried listening to an audio version, but found it akin to wearing the sunglasses; it kept the story at a distance, untouchable, too far for it to work the magic she knew simmered just behind the words. Perhaps when her eyes finally gave up, the book would fade away too, and she wouldn't have to face all that she had lost.

She went around the garden a second time—*sixteen paces, four steps, sixteen paces*—and saw someone standing at the door to the shed. She strained her eyes against the darkness in her periphery and made out Mr Fitzpatrick, looking down at his shoes like an awkward schoolboy.

He brightened as she came up to him. "Good morning, Dr Murphy."

"Hello, Mr Fitzpatrick. Did we have an appointment?" She frantically thought back to her notebook, wondering if she might have missed some note in the margin, too close to the paper's edge, just out of reach.

"No, nothing like that. I just wanted to stop by and thank you for the recommendations. I've been feeling much better, and so has Fiona. She's been asking for more Jerry Spinelli."

"That's wonderful." Victoria shaded her eyes with her hand, even though the day was grey.

"And do you know what? The lout's been calling her night and day begging for another chance. I don't know what on earth's got into him, but Fiona won't hear anything about it. Says she has no room in her future for small-minded people. What do you make of that?"

"Good for her," she said warmly. "Love isn't easy at that age—at any age, I suppose. But she has a good head. Takes after her father."

Mr Fitzpatrick blushed. "Yes. Well. I just wanted to say thank you again." He waved goodbye and let himself out through the back gate.

Victoria returned to the house, ate her lunch in the breakfast nook, and brought out her eye drops. She wasn't sure if there was any point, now; she'd forgotten to ask Dr Blythe if she should still bother taking them. Still, even holding onto one more day was worth the trouble. Even one more hour.

She let the medicine drip into her eyes, then lay back on the sofa and began counting one hundred and twenty seconds. She'd reached seventy-eight when her phone rang.

She lifted herself up, keeping her eyes squeezed tightly closed, and felt around for her phone. It clattered to the floor by her feet. She picked it up and stabbed the screen with her fingers a few times until she heard it connect.

"Hello?"

"Dr Murphy?"

She was holding it upside down. She fumbled the phone into place. "Yes. Is this Natalia?" Victoria recognised the distinctive accent.

"I hope I do not bother you. I call only to say thank you for recommending me the book. I liked reading it very much."

"You're welcome. I hope it's helping," Victoria said. She had lost count of the seconds. She manoeuvred herself back into a lying position.

"Yes! And do you know what happened? After, I went to bring it back to the library, and I spoke to someone who came there looking for the same one. She is from Poland, but she has family in Russia, just like me. And tomorrow we are going to get a coffee."

Victoria's eyes were beginning to sting. She opened them, blinking away the last of the eye drops. "That's great, Natalia. I'm happy you're doing better."

"Anyway, thank you for telling me the book. It is for you I have a new friend."

Natalia said goodbye and hung up the phone.

The next day, Victoria went back into the garden. *Four steps down.* A light rain was beginning to fall. A new client was coming in for a consultation at one o'clock, but until then she was determined to imbibe every detail with every moment she had left.

A man stood outside the clinic. At first she thought Mr Fitzpatrick had come back, but no—this man was slighter, his hair dark. It was Dr Blythe.

"Good morning, Dr Blythe. Are you looking for an appointment?" she said, only half teasing. The doctor looked as out of place among the roses and thyme as she felt inside the cold, stark walls of his clinic.

"Just came to see how you were doing." He shifted from one foot to another.

Victoria wasn't sure she believed him, though she was glad he was there. "Would you like to come in?"

She unlocked the door to the shed, suddenly self-conscious of the fading yellow roses and overstuffed armchairs and cramped walls that barely allowed space enough for two. He followed her in, and she busied herself putting the kettle on so she wouldn't have to look at him. But then, she reminded herself, that was ridiculous. Very soon she would never be able to look at him again.

Since there was nothing more to occupy her hands with, she sat in one of the chairs and waited for the water. Dr Blythe took the other. Unlike Mr Fitzpatrick, he was just the right size.

"I've been hearing some interesting things about you, Miss Murphy."

"About me?" Though he said it mildly, Victoria tensed. Small-town gossip was rarely kind. "What sort of trouble have I been getting into?"

"Geoffrey Lawlins came in yesterday, with his sister. I think you know her?"

"Yes, Mrs Haverton. Of course. How are they doing? It must be so difficult for them."

"Well," Dr Blythe crossed his legs, and uncrossed them again. "Geoffrey's been reading, apparently. I'll never again say I don't believe in miracles."

Victoria hid a smile. "Perhaps he's reassessing his priorities."

"That's not all," said Dr Blythe. "Our oncologist took a look at him, and it seems his tumour's starting to respond to the treatment at last. It's the strangest thing."

"That's wonderful news." She wondered what was taking the kettle so long. "I'm glad to hear that Geoffrey Lawlins is made of stronger stuff than any of us knew."

Dr Blythe studied her for a moment. "I'll remember not to underestimate him."

The kettle began to whistle gently on the hob. Victoria stood and poured tea for the two of them. She brought the teapot to the table and handed him a teacup.

"So how does all this…your practice work, Miss— Dr Murphy?"

"Oh, well, it's simple really." She nestled back into the chair. "People come when they need someone to talk to, and I listen, and then I suggest something to read."

"Is that all?"

Victoria took a sip of her tea. "Never doubt the power of a good story, Dr Blythe."

He put down his teacup. "Alright. What would you recommend for me?"

"I didn't know you were much of a reader."

"'Course I am. I grew up reading. In fact, reading Patrick Taylor is what made me want to study medicine."

"Is it really?" Victoria grinned, and some of her tension melted away. Patrick Taylor's *Irish Country Doctor* books had got her through some difficult winter nights. "Is it like you imagined it'd be?"

Dr Blythe shrugged self-consciously. "Life isn't always like it is in the stories."

"Stranger than fiction, I hear." Victoria put down her teacup and leaned forward. "Tell me, Dr Blythe, what malady are you hoping to read away today?"

"Well," he said, "Dr Murphy. I'm worried about a friend. An acquaintance, really, but I've become quite fond of her. She's just had some terrible news, and I don't know how to help." He looked down and picked at his cuffs. "My entire career is meant to be about helping people, and I'm completely powerless."

"There was nothing more you could have done." Victoria reached across the table and grasped his hand. She did it without thinking, and the physical contact startled her. "I used to think stories could fix everything. Until my mum…and, you know." She waved her other hand towards her eyes. "But I help people. At least, I try. Some days that feels like enough."

A book flashed behind her eyes, there and gone so quickly she almost missed it.

"I thought I'd get used to it, in time," said Dr Blythe. "The ones you can't save. The illnesses you can't stop. But…"

"I know," she said. "It's okay."

There it was again—Dr Blythe's book. She sucked in a breath, her hand tightening. This time there could be no mistaking it.

A Little Princess.

"Maybe," she said slowly, "maybe there is one more thing you can do."

It was strange having Dr Blythe inside her house. Aside from herself, no one had been in it for years. Yet somehow, the emptiness didn't feel quite so vast with him beside her. She led him to the sitting room and handed Dr Blythe the book, the one her father had read to her on those long, terrifying nights while they waited for word from the hospital. His voice kept the darkness away.

Victoria lay back on the sofa and closed her eyes. She heard the fluttering of pages as he opened the book, the rustle of his fingers against the old cloth. Then he began to read.

"*Once, on a dark winter's day...*" Dr Blythe's voice settled over her like a blanket. "*...when the yellow fog hung so thick and heavy in the streets of London that the lamps were lighted and the shop windows blazed with gas as they do at night, an odd-looking little girl sat in a cab with her father...*"

And Victoria smiled as the shadows slowly receded and the world unfurled into shape.

Acknowledgments

I've been very lucky to connect with so many wonderful writers and booklovers who have helped bring this collection to life. I'd like to extend my gratitude to Archna Sharma, Alison Savage, and the rest of the team at Neem Tree Press; Rebecca Purton, whose wonderful artwork adorns the pages of this book; the writers whose input has helped make these stories the best they can be, including but not limited to Ann Adams, Carlo Gébler, Nessa Mahoney, Emma Mooney, Elisabeth Moore, Jo B, Dawn Miller, and Fiona Picard; and finally, all the beautiful, terrible, inspiring, insightful, narcissistic, degenerate, compassionate, cruel, kind, altruistic, and wonderfully weird people I've met over the years who have given me a wealth of life experience to write about. Taking memories and turning them into stories is the most powerful alchemy there is, and I could not have done it alone. Thank you all for being a part of this journey.

About the Author

Fija Callaghan is a storyteller and poet who has been recognised by a number of awards, including shortlisting for the HG Wells Short Story Prize. Her writing can be found in venues like *Seaside Gothic*, *Gingerbread House*, *Howl: New Irish Writing*, and elsewhere. Her debut collection of fabulist short stories, *Frail Little Embers*, was created to inspire hope in times of darkness. You can find out more about her at www.fijacallaghan.com.